THE
SECRET
OF
WINDTHORN

Also by Bea Carlton
in Large Print:

Terror in the Night
Deadly Gypsy Blue
In the Foxes' Lair
In the House of the Enemy
Moonshell
Voices from the Mist

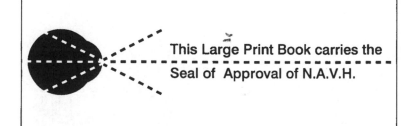

This Large Print Book carries the
Seal of Approval of N.A.V.H.

THE
SECRET
OF
WINDTHORN

Bea Carlton

Thorndike Press • Waterville, Maine

Published in 2004 by arrangement with Bea Carlton.

Thorndike Press® Large Print Christian Mystery.

The tree indicium is a trademark of Thorndike Press.

The text of this Large Print edition is unabridged.
Other aspects of the book may vary from the original edition.

Set in 16 pt. Plantin by Elena Picard.

Printed in the United States on permanent paper.

Library of Congress Cataloging-in-Publication Data

Carlton, Bea.
    The secret of Windthorn / Bea Carlton.
        p. cm.
    Sequel to: Terror in the night.
    Summary: While a blizzard rages outside, Joy Kyle and
Carole Loring discover a storm of another kind raging
within the walls of Windthorn, as the disappearance of a
priceless, ancient scroll creates a catalyst of terror — and
faith.
    ISBN 0-7862-5707-5 (lg. print : hc : alk. paper)
    1. Large type books. [1. Christian life — Fiction.
2. Mystery and detective stories. 3. Large type books.]
I. Title.
PZ7.C21685Se 2004
    [Fic]—dc22   2003054241

Dedicated with much love
to our daughter, Rebecca:
the joy of our life,
and to her husband, Newton:
the son we never had.

As the Founder/CEO of NAVH, the only national health agency solely devoted to those who, although not totally blind, have an eye disease which could lead to serious visual impairment, I am pleased to recognize Thorndike Press* as one of the leading publishers in the large print field.

Founded in 1954 in San Francisco to prepare large print textbooks for partially seeing children, NAVH became the pioneer and standard setting agency in the preparation of large type.

Today, those publishers who meet our standards carry the prestigious "Seal of Approval" indicating high quality large print. We are delighted that Thorndike Press is one of the publishers whose titles meet these standards. We are also pleased to recognize the significant contribution Thorndike Press is making in this important and growing field.

Lorraine H. Marchi, L.H.D.
Founder/CEO
NAVH

* Thorndike Press encompasses the following imprints: Thorndike, Wheeler, Walker and Large Print Press.

1

Skye Windthorn paused at the edge of the trail which led to a side door of his huge, windswept house. The faint sound of skis arrested his movement. The dark-haired man, tall and sparely built, appeared to be about thirty years old. His slate-grey eyes narrowed. After cocking his head to one side in a listening stance, he muttered in disgust, turned, and crunched back across the snow to where he could get a clear view of the hill he had just ascended.

A dark scowl creased his lean, stern face and his eyes glinted with anger. Two brightly garbed skiers were sweeping down the opposite slope, circling large fir and spruce trees in the park-like expanse of glistening snow. His lips curled into an unconscious display of contempt as he observed that both skiers were women.

For perhaps the hundredth time he wished fervently that he had not sold part of his property to Jeffrey Pitman for the exclusive, year-round resort. Forest Lakes Lodge. He had needed the money badly but for two years now his privacy had been invaded by skiers — male and female — who either inadvertently or purposely used part of his own private skiing slopes instead of staying on Pitman property.

The two women skiers had reached the bottom of the hill and were now working their way up the gentle slope toward him. Through narrowed eyes, Skye saw that both were young. One, a petite brunette, was dressed in a red and silver ski suit that set off her unusual beauty. The other, blonde hair framing a pixie face, was garbed in blue and yellow. The brunette was obviously an excellent skier while the blonde was apparently not as comfortable on the skis.

The brunette came to a skillful stop not far from Skye and called out a cheerful, "Hi," before turning toward her companion, who had stopped close by.

Obviously satisfied that the other young woman had come to a safe halt, the dark-headed beauty walked on her skis to a position nearer Skye who had not acknowledged her greeting with even a curt nod.

"I'm Carole Loring and this is my friend

Joy Kyle. We're staying at Forest Lakes Lodge," she said with a smile.

Skye's grey eyes smoldered with anger and his voice was testy. "Are you ladies aware of the fact that you are trespassing?"

Skye felt a grim satisfaction when his words caused a faint flush to rise in the lovely face of the brunette.

But the young woman's level gaze met his hostile glare coolly. "No, we didn't know we were off the resort property. I'm sorry."

Skye had ignored the blonde woman until she stated, almost as if to herself, "You're Skye Windthorn, the former owner of the land Jeffrey built his resort on."

"The same," Skye said brusquely.

"We'll give him your regards," the dark haired beauty said, a slight twinkle in her voice.

Annoyed, Skye said rudely, "If I want any correspondence with Pitman, I can do it myself."

Carole did not act in the least intimidated. Rather, her calm, blue-black eyes seemed to be assessing him as if to determine what kind of strange creature he was. "Good day, Mr. Windthorn," she finally said. "I'm sorry we intruded on your property." Abruptly she turned to her companion, "Shall we go, Joy?"

Skye observed that though the dark-eyed, dark-haired woman was smaller, her companion had a frailer, more delicate look. His lips curled with scorn as his cold eyes took in her soft, blonde prettiness: full, petal-soft lips, clear pink and white complexion and gentle, sky blue eyes. *The helpless, pampered kind of female that I detest the most,* he thought maliciously.

Before the blonde — who appeared to be disconcerted by his baleful, derisive stare — could turn around on her skis, a deep, gruff bark sounded from the line of trees behind and above Skye. Almost instantly a huge, dark brindled Great Dane, gleaming white teeth bared, came leaping and bounding through the deep snow, growling fiercely.

Skye more sensed than saw the two women trying to get their skis in position to flee down the hill away from the awesome creature bearing down upon them. A malevolent smile tugged at the corners of his arrogant, well-chiseled lips, deepening the cleft in his chin.

Just as the dog would have leaped past him, Skye spoke one word sharply. "Stop!" The hurtling creature plowed to a halt and moved quickly to stand at the tall man's side. Skye rested a long-fingered, scholarly

10

hand on the dog's head and the dog turned adoring eyes upon his master's face briefly before he again looked toward the women. A low, threatening rumble sounded deep in his throat.

When the dark-haired beauty glanced back nervously, Skye raised his voice to call mockingly, "As you can see, Prince doesn't like trespassers either!"

Chuckling without mirth, the man watched the women glide away down the gentle slope and start up the opposite hillside before he turned away. Then he moved smoothly along the trail with the dog bounding over the snow ahead of him. Several minutes later they reached the edge of the clearing that separated his house from the forest. He snapped the skis free of his boots, and placed them and the ski poles across one shoulder before moving down a cleared path toward the house.

"That's two that we've seen the last of, Prince," he said companionably to the Great Dane, who dashed back to push his cold nose into his master's mittened hand.

At that moment the voice of a man in a dark suit called from the doorway of the enclosed porch. "Mr. Windthorn, there's someone on the phone for you!"

Skye moved quickly onto the porch and

11

began to remove his ski boots. "Who is it, Washington?"

"The sheriff, I think."

Skye poked his feet into house slippers before crossing the room into the warmth of the large kitchen. Prince followed and immediately took possession of a woolly rug in front of the blazing log in the fireplace.

Picking up the telephone, Skye said, "Windthorn here."

A few minutes later Skye hung up the phone and turned to his housekeeper. "That cat burglar has robbed another mansion in our area — Ridgecrest. You know, the one about ten miles from here."

"That's getting close. Isn't that three burglaries this month? What's the sheriff's department doing that they haven't caught the guy?"

Skye took down a heavy mug, filled it with coffee, added cream, and carried it to the oilcloth-covered kitchen table before he answered. Seating himself, he sampled the coffee and then stirred it thoughtfully.

"Sheriff Scott says they are doing everything possible but there just aren't any leads. There's never a trace of anything to go on, no fingerprints, no tracks — nothing! And no one has ever gotten a

12

glimpse of him. Every time he's entered a home, he's slipped in and out as silently as a ghost."

Washington added, "The paper's been calling him the Midnight Cat Burglar." Then he said soberly, "I don't like him prowling around our area while we have that extremely valuable scroll you're working on in the house."

"I was thinking of the scroll, too," Skye said. "But I lock it in my desk if I have to leave for even a minute. That heavy oak desk would be pretty hard to break into."

"I know, sir, but it still bothers me having something that valuable in the house."

"I'm not really that concerned," Skye said to his housekeeper. "So far our cat burglar has taken only jewelry and money. An ancient leather scroll like this would be hard to dispose of."

"Ransom for a rare treasure like that could be a temptation," Washington reasoned.

"Yes," Skye said slowly, sipping his coffee. "That is something to consider. We'll have to take every precaution. Tell Kim to be extra alert. I hope to be finished with the scroll within the next few months, and I'll admit it will be a relief to get it safely back to Egypt where it belongs."

Skye set his coffee cup down. "By the way, that marble paperweight is missing from my office again."

Washington raised his head from the sink where he was cleaning vegetables. His keen eyes met Skye's gravely, "I retrieved it and put it back on your desk." An unspoken understanding passed between them.

Skye sighed deeply. "Thank you, Washington. I suspected that's where it had gone." His grey eyes looked troubled. For a second, he seemed about to say more as Washington stood quiet, his hands still upon the edges of the sink. Then Skye heaved another sigh and rose. "I'd better get to work." He strode from the room.

Washington stood deep in thought for a long moment before he rang for Kim and gave him Skye's instructions.

2

The logs in the huge stone fireplace in the main dining room of Forest Lakes Lodge crackled and hissed, throwing out heat and lending an air of comfort and warmth. The wind outside moaned and shrieked, driving snow against the windows and piling it into drifts in the driveways and parking area. But the dining room denied the storm outside. Relaxing and cozy, it was brightened by the laughter and animated talking of the diners scattered throughout the room at candle bedecked, polished oak tables.

Trim, efficient waitresses, uniformed in the resort's colors of red and cream, wove their way between the tables. After a day of skiing in the bright cold of Idaho's snowy wonderland, the food and the cheeriness radiating from the fireplace were thoroughly appreciated.

Joy Kyle paused in the wide dining room doorway and searched the room until she located her friends, Carole and David Loring, sitting at a table. Her heart quickened with affection. David, vibrantly alive and good looking with a thatch of unruly red-gold hair and keen blue eyes, was so obviously in love with Carole that it put a lump in Joy's throat whenever she saw them together.

And Carole. Joy's eyes misted suddenly as they studied her friend. Carole was beautiful with her glowing dark eyes, lustrous black curls, and petite gracefulness. But Joy knew her charm was not just outward. The real person inside was just as genuine and beautiful and caring.

Just then she saw Carole wave. As Joy made her way through the maze of tables to join them, happiness bubbled up inside her. It was still almost more than her mind could comprehend how God had used this couple who were unknown to her twelve months ago to bring about a reconciliation between her and her father, the wealthy and talented artist Charles Prentice.

Just two months before, Charles had married Carole's spritely grandmother, Margaret, and brought her to Forest Lakes Lodge for their honeymoon. They had fallen in love with the resort and Charles had invited Carole, David, Joy and her five-year-old daughter, Mitzi, here for Christmas as his guests. It was to be the first Christmas in many years that Joy had spent with her father.

David rose to pull out a chair for Joy. "You were so long in coming to dinner we had begun to wonder if you and Jeffrey had eloped." David's blue eyes were twinkling.

Joy joined in Carole and David's good-natured laughter but felt her face grow warm with an odd mixture of pleasure and embarrassment.

"He hasn't even asked me yet," she said archly.

"He will! He will! Just think what it will be like to be married to Jeffrey Pitman, the owner of Forest Lakes Lodge, and live in this glorious setting all the time."

Joy made a face at David. She knew she should be used to David's teasing but because she had, to a large degree, isolated herself from people since her unfortunate marriage, she was unaccustomed to the easy bantering of friends. Also, it was still a new thought that she was free to accept the attentions of a highly eligible young bachelor such as Jeffrey Pitman.

"Stop teasing Joy," Carole commanded her husband good-naturedly. Turning back to Joy, she spoke wistfully, "I miss Mitzi

17

and she's only been gone for a few hours."

"So do I — dreadfully," Joy sighed. "But I just couldn't refuse Dad's pleas to let Mitzi go with him and your grandmother to San Diego. He was so distressed that he had to run off like this, but when he said his business trip would become a pleasure trip if Mitzi could go, I couldn't refuse. They want to take her to Sea World and to the zoo there, and other things as well. But it will be a long two weeks without her."

"Your dad and Gran look so happy together," Carole said softly. "I'm so glad for them. I know it's been lonely for them both. My grandfather died when I was only four and Gran never remarried. Perhaps she was too busy making a home for me."

"I'm very happy for them, too. But I can't help wishing that Dad had come to know the Lord years ago." Joy's eyes held a far-away look. "Things would have been so different for Mother before she died."

"I know how you feel," Carole said gently.

A pretty waitress appeared at their table to take their order. Joy gave her order abstractedly. Her mind was still on her father and their lives before Joy left home.

When the waitress moved away, Joy asked, "Can you imagine what it was like

18

for Mother?" Joy grimaced as if in physical pain. "The loneliness, the awful loneliness!" She shivered, "I can still feel it. As I grew older it became a huge, aching void inside me that longed and thirsted and hungered for the companionship of other young people. When I ran away, Daddy forbade me to ever return."

"Charles has paid a heavy penalty in remorse," Carole said gently. "And God does forgive."

"I know," Joy's smile was tremulous. "And I have forgiven him, too. But it hasn't been easy, believe me. It took a lot of prayer before I could forgive him. And by God's help I can now even say I forgive my husband. He was a cruel, violent man and he never loved me, but I can thank God for the one good thing our marriage brought to me . . ."

"Mitzi," Carole finished.

"Yes, Mitzi," Joy said. "She has been such a joy to my life!"

Suddenly Joy's sweet face looked troubled and her blue eyes seemed to darken as she searched the faces of David and Carole. "When Ferron died eight months ago, I was glad. Is that wrong?" She hurried on before they could answer. "I was terrified of him and lived in fear that he would return — especially after Mitzi was born."

David's voice was warm and reassuring, "Joy, it is only natural that you would feel relief when the menace to your lives was removed. Don't feel guilty. Just be thankful that God kept you both safe from him. And the quicker you put those unhappy days behind you, the better," he finished decisively.

"I'm trying to." Joy looked contrite. "I'm sorry to be a wet blanket."

"You aren't," Carole said emphatically.

"How are the ski lessons coming?" David asked.

"I wish I was progressing faster, and I suppose with a lot more practice I'll master it after a while," Joy sighed. "But Mitzi took to skiing like a bird to flying."

"You're doing fine!" Carole declared stoutly. "After all, you knew very little about either downhill or cross-country skiing when you got here two weeks ago."

"I heartily agree!" The rejoinder came from a bearded, smiling young man of about twenty-eight who had just approached their table. The slightly stout, well-dressed owner of Forest Lakes Resort stood smiling happily at his friends.

"Jeff, sit down and join us for dinner,"

David invited cordially.

"If you're sure I'm not intruding, I'd love to," Jeffrey said.

"We'd love to have you," David assured him as Carole and Joy smiled their welcome.

Jeffrey signaled a hovering waiter who quickly brought another chair and took his employer's order.

After a waitress had brought steaming mugs of hot chocolate and departed, David addressed Jeffrey. "What's this I hear about a cat burglar in this area?"

Carole's eyes widened in surprise and she exclaimed, "A cat burglar! Here?"

"Not here at Forest Lakes Resort," Jeffrey protested quickly. "But there has been a burglary at a mansion in our area. Where did you hear about it, David? The sheriff's department just called me about it a while ago."

"One of your lodgers has a Scanner; he heard about it on that. He also said this cat burglar has been burglarizing a home a month for the past six months but that this month . . ."

". . . there have been three," Jeffrey finished. He groaned. "That's young Ramsey Blake you were talking to. I'll have to have a talk with him or he'll have everyone afraid to go to sleep tonight for fear the cat burglar will sneak in and slit their throats. He gets all the crime news on that Scanner and then tells it to everyone he meets."

"Is it true that there has been a burglary?" Joy asked.

"I'm afraid so."

"Has the resort ever been burglarized by this cat burglar?" David asked.

"One of our clients was a few months ago," Jeffrey admitted. "As you know, we insist that all valuables be placed in our vault. But this lady refused to do so and the cat burglar took her jewels right out of her room while she was asleep."

"Were they recovered?" Carole asked.

"No," Jeffrey answered. "The odd thing about these burglaries is that nothing that has been stolen has ever surfaced." He grimaced. "And, as our news informant told you, the burglaries have been going on for about six months."

"Maybe that's why he hasn't been caught," David said. "If he had sold them, there would be others in on it. As it is, there is only one clever thief involved. Maybe he plans to leave the area before he tries to dispose of them."

"Does the sheriff's department have any idea who could be doing the burglarizing?" Carole questioned.

"None at all! They're calling him the Midnight Cat Burglar because he always does his work after midnight. It's a good name for him. He not only enters through the upper part of the house, but he is as quiet as a cat."

"That's creepy. Imagine waking up to find a strange man ransacking your room — or that he had been there and gone while you slept." Joy shuddered.

Jeffrey turned his warm hazel eyes toward Joy. "Don't worry, this cat burglar is a thief, but he has never physically harmed anyone. Besides, we have tightened up our security here at the resort on all fronts."

At that moment two trim, tray-laden waitresses arrived, cutting off their conversation about burglars.

"This is some place you have here," David said a few minutes later as they began to eat. "Beautiful country and splendid ski runs."

Jeffrey's brown eyes lighted with quiet pride. "I was very fortunate to obtain this property. It not only has excellent ski slopes, but the fishing and scenery are fantastic all year 'round. Even with the prices I must charge to maintain this place in the excellence I strive for, we scarcely ever have rooms that aren't filled."

"Your food *is* outstanding," Joy interposed.

Jeffrey Pitman looked pleased. "Thanks! I'm glad you like everything."

"Oh, we don't like everything!" Carole said.

Startled, the resort owner's head turned quickly toward Carole. Then, seeing the teasing light in Carole's eyes, he smiled, "And what don't you like?"

"Your neighbor," Carole said lightly. "Or maybe I should say your neighbor doesn't like Joy and me."

"I'll second that!" Joy ejaculated. "I thought he was going to let that monster of a dog tear us limb from limb!"

Comprehension dawned suddenly in Jeffrey's eyes. His smile faded. "You mean Skye Windthorn," he said slowly.

Alarm registered in David's blue eyes, "Where was this? Out on the ski runs?"

"We trespassed on Mr. Skye Windthorn's precious property," Joy stated. "We didn't realize it, of course, but that ogre of a man set us straight quickly. I never saw such rudeness!"

"He didn't set his dog on you?" asked Jeffrey incredulously, his eyes mirroring David's concern.

"No," Carole admitted. "We had just

skied down a slope and saw a man standing at the top of the next little slope watching us, so we went over to him to say 'hi.' Everyone is so friendly here at the lodge, and I presumed he was a lodge guest. But he never even bothered to return our greeting, just informed us in no uncertain terms that we were trespassing."

Joy took up the story. "And about that time the biggest dog I ever saw in my life came tearing out of the woods, growling and snarling and running straight for us. I was so scared, I thought I'd die of fright before he even got to us!" She shuddered in remembrance.

"But Skye called him off before he touched you, didn't he?" questioned Jeffrey.

"Yes, but that hateful man never said a word to the dog until it was almost upon us. I'm sure he meant to frighten us," Carole replied. "But just before the dog reached us, the man ordered him to stop and he stopped so suddenly he literally plowed into the snow."

"Did Skye say anything else to you?" Jeffrey asked.

"He called as we were leaving — as fast as we could get underway — 'Prince doesn't like trespassers either!'" Joy answered.

"Sounds like a threat," David said. "Who is this Skye — what did you say his name was?"

Jeffrey's face was grave. "Skye Windthorn. His estate joins Forest Lakes Lodge. In fact, I purchased most of this property from him. I'm sure he would never have sold if he hadn't been in a financial bind, and I'm equally certain he regrets selling his land to a resort."

Jeffrey stroked his short brown beard reflectively and frowned. His deep-set brown eyes mirrored more than a casual concern. "Skye Windthorn is a strange man and his actions sometimes worry me. If any of our skiers venture onto his property, he makes it as unpleasant for them as possible. I even wonder if he might be dangerous."

Joy looked shocked and Carole asked incredulously, "Jeff, you aren't serious, surely?"

Jeff suddenly smiled. "I expect I am taking his actions a little too seriously. The man is just anti-social and I'm sure it annoys him to have his privacy invaded. I'm sorry, ladies, if he gave you a scare."

David leaned toward Jeffrey. "Skye Windthorn . . . that name rings a bell, but I can't place where I've heard it before. Is he well-known for something?"

"Yes, Skye is well-known in some circles. He is an authority on ancient writings. I understand that he's an expert at deciphering archaeological findings, doing some of the work at Windthorn and at other times flying to various ruins and museums to work."

Joy wrinkled her nose. "Sounds like dull, dusty work."

"Not really," Jeffrey said. "Archaeology is a fascinating field and although a lot of it is tedious, exacting work, it is also exciting to find out how other people lived, thought and progressed."

David, a lover of study, quickly backed him up. "I agree. There was a time, before I settled on biology and decided to be a teacher, that I considered entering the field of archaeology."

Carole suddenly spoke up. "This Windthorn fellow sounds like quite a character. What else do you know about him?"

"Not much. He's a very private person," Jeffrey answered. "He lives in a huge old fortress-like mansion that was built by his grandfather. A creepy place built of a dark grey, almost black, stone that has always been called Windthorn.

"His father was something of a loner too,

a scholar of some reputation. He was a historian and wrote a number of books on ancient cultures. He was world-traveled and wealthy from a fortune he inherited from his father and which he passed down to his only child, Skye Windthorn."

"No one mentions a woman," Carole said thoughtfully. "Is this Skye married; is there a mother or children at Windthorn?"

"There are no women or children at Windthorn. Two men-servants take care of the house and its master," Jeffrey supplied. "Windthorn men seem to have been poor judges of women, at least the last two were. And I think the women they have been involved with is the cause for Skye's antisocial complex. His mother was a pretty, blonde socialite, flitting here and there. Skye was placed in a boarding school, out of her way and out of the way of his writer, researcher father."

"I can relate to Skye in that!" Carole said "My parents did the same thing to me. It hurts to be shuttled away from those you want most to love you."

"I remember Skye's father," Jeffrey said thoughtfully. "Not well, of course. He was a gentle, scholarly looking man, as I recall. He gave one the feeling that he lived in a world all his own so I expect he would have been a poor husband — and father. His wife ran away with a colorful Italian guest at Windthorn whom she had only known for a week. Skye was twelve at the time.

"And Skye married a butterfly socialite, too," Jeffrey finished. "Every bit as blonde, pretty and bubbleheaded as his capricious mother. They could have been cut from the same piece of cloth. She ran away with Skye's closest friend one night in Skye's private plane. They were taking off from the small airfield on Windthorn property when the plane crashed and killed them both."

"How horrible!" Carole exclaimed.

"And their only child, a little boy, was killed too," Jeffrey added. "A tragic family!"

"The poor man," Joy said. "At least I can understand a little bit why he is so bitter."

Jeffrey looked across the table at Joy and smiled the slow smile that turned his almost homely face into an attractive one. "Don't waste your sympathy on him. He wouldn't like it. Now I'm a different kinda fellow. I appreciate all the attention a certain pretty blonde can give me."

Joy smiled and a becoming pink tinged her fair face as she dropped her eyes in confusion. She had been separated from her husband for a long time before he'd died, but she had been scrupulously faithful to him and had avoided any social contact with men. But even now that Ferron was dead, Joy still had not dated, so she hardly knew how to respond to the attention of an admirer.

Jeffrey Pitman, the successful, bachelor owner of Forest Lakes Lodge had made no secret of the fact that he had been attracted to Joy since she had first arrived two weeks before. Joy found the attention flattering but rather unsettling, too. She liked his company — he was witty, entertaining, self-assured, and thoughtful. He was even a Christian, but she was wary of an emotional relationship at this point. And he was coming on a little too fast and a little too strong. She didn't know quite how to handle it.

She was glad the two waitresses returned to exchange their soup bowls for the main course, taking the attention away from her.

As they were eating, David again brought up the subject of Skye Windthorn. Turning to his wife he said, "Honey, what kind of dog did this Windthorn guy have?"

Carole's blue-black eyes narrowed in thought. "He was very big and a dark brindle color with pointed ears like they had been cropped. . . ."

"He's an extremely large, purebred Great Dane," Jeffrey interposed. "I've made his acquaintance, too. When Skye and I were working out the details of this property sale, he was always along with Skye in the car. And the one time I went to Windthorn to transact business, Prince was right behind Skye when he let me into his house.

"I tried to make friends with him because I like dogs, but he refused to have anything to do with me. Obviously he dislikes people as much as his owner. But one thing I can say, he obeys Skye's every command by voice or hand signal. He's exceptionally well-trained and obedient."

David frowned slightly and then asked, "Jeff, you said a while ago you thought Skye Windthorn might be dangerous. In what way?"

Every eye was on Jeffrey who hesitated before he answered, "I'm not sure. Perhaps I'm imagining things, but there is something about the man that troubles me. Carole and Joy are not the first guests that he has been very nasty to. I'm considering putting a high fence on his side of my property. The safety of Forest Lakes

31

lodgers is my responsibility. I hope he wouldn't actually harm anyone, but he is a strange man. And it alarms me to think what might happen if someone came upon that dog when Skye wasn't around!"

His eyes went to Joy. "There are bright flags that mark the line between Forest Lakes Lodge and Windthorn property. You and Carole be careful to stay on this side of the line of flags."

"You can be sure we'll stay on the right side of that line from now on!" Joy promised him.

3

By the next morning the snowstorm had blown itself out. The bare branches of the aspen, and the deep green and blue-green limbs of the different evergreen trees wore a heavy frosting of superlative white, resplendent under the sparkling cold light of the sun. Its breathtaking beauty soon lured most of the lodgers outside to revel in the cold magic of the snow.

It was a perfect day for skiing. The Lorings and Joy took to the slopes early but after about two hours, David went back to the lodge to study. He had returned to college this fall to earn his teaching certificate, which would require two more semesters of study. College was not as easy for David this time. Even on Christmas vacation at the resort, he spent some time nearly every morning in study.

As David left the ski run, Joy was just coming from her lesson. She joined Carole and they spent the remainder of the morning together, going through the various techniques Joy was learning and then just skiing for pleasure.

During lunch, David spoke apologetically to Carole, "I'm nearly finished with that thesis — the rough draft, that is — and I need to work on it a couple of hours this afternoon while it's rolling through my mind so well. Can you. . . ."

Annoyance flashed across Carole's expressive face. "David, I thought this was to be a vacation!"

David studied Carole's resentful face for a long moment before he answered, "You're right, this is supposed to be a vacation. And besides, it isn't fair to you that I have my head in a book all the time. I'll finish it tomorrow."

Carole was instantly remorseful. "David, I know you lack just a little on your thesis. Perhaps it would be better if you finished it while it is fresh in your mind. I need to write some letters anyway."

But David was adamant and insisted on spending the afternoon with his wife. They decided to go on an ice-fishing outing Jeffrey had planned for the afternoon. Jeffrey had already asked Joy to come with him — their first real date — and she had consented. Several snowmobiles would transport the fishing party.

Carole thrilled to the rush of the icy, pungent, fir-scented wind in her face and to the exhilarating snowmobile ride, but the feeling that she wasn't being fair to David kept nibbling at her conscience.

Carole acknowledged that teaching was David's passion, and she tried hard not to resent the time he spent in class and study. But David would never know the battles she fought in prayer to keep her resolve of not being a hindrance to his chosen vocation and calling. When she had seen that he was bringing his books on their Christmas vacation, she had had to bite her tongue to keep back a sarcastic remark.

But I am also concerned about David, she thought. *He looks so tired and strained. I'm sure he is overtaxing himself.*

Carole's remorse was short-lived when she saw how David enjoyed the new challenge of fishing through holes cut in the ice. He was a skillful fisherman and soon had several wriggling whitefish in his creel. It seemed almost like magic to Carole when she saw the tiredness vanish from his face and his blue eyes take on their old sparkle. His shouts of unrestrained glee when he landed a fish erased the last vestiges of Carole's guilt.

That night, back at the lodge when they joined a group around the fireplace where a guitar-playing country singer was entertaining, David leaned over and whispered to Carole, "I'm surely glad you rescued me. I didn't realize how tired I was until I really relaxed out there at the lake this afternoon. I was wound up as tight as an alarm clock! After I finish the rough copy of that thesis tomorrow morning, I promise to not open another book until I get back home!"

"I'm glad," Carole said, her eyes glowing with pleasure.

Carole suddenly caught sight of Joy across the room and smiled. She and Jeffrey were laughing together at something he had just whispered to her. As Carole watched, Jeffrey reached for Joy's hand and Joy didn't object. As the two turned their attention back to the singers, Carole's heart quickened. She had seen the glow in Joy's pale cheeks.

The next morning David joined Carole and Joy on the downhill ski runs for a couple of hours before he went in to work. The weatherman on the radio predicted snow by night, but the bright sun on the ski slopes made them doubt the accuracy of his forecast.

"I should have that thesis in good shape by noon and all packed away for the duration of our vacation," David promised cheerfully as he left to go study. He planted a kiss on Carole's lips and went whistling away.

Pleased, Carole turned back and watched Joy come gliding toward her. Joy made a perfect stop with a stem christie maneuver and when Carole applauded, she laughed in breathless pleasure.

"I'm finally getting the knack, I do believe!"

"You're doing great!" Carole agreed. "Say, why don't we change to cross-country skis and go over to the line of flags at the resort property line. Maybe we can see the Windthorn mansion."

Joy looked doubtful. "It's quite a ways over there and the news said snow was coming. Besides, we were closer than the line of flags the other time and we didn't see a house, just a line of heavy forest."

"But we would come in from a different angle this time," Carole reasoned. "I don't know why, but I'm curious about the Windthorn family and their spooky old house. We'd be careful to stay on the lodge property so there shouldn't be any problem. I guess old houses just fascinate me. It would be good experience for you," she said persuasively, "and it really isn't so far."

Joy looked up at the sky. "Clouds are beginning to gather," she said uneasily. "Do you think it's wise?"

"I'm sure we can beat the snow," Carole said gaily. "Let's go!"

Reluctantly Joy agreed. Stopping only long enough to change to cross-country skis and lighter clothing, they were soon skimming across steep slopes. Joy found cross-country skiing exhilarating. She had spent a lot of time in practice, and now it was paying off. She shrugged off her apprehensions and allowed herself to enjoy the day and the exercise.

So absorbed was she in her skiing and in following Carole's lead that they were almost to the line of flags, waving gaily in the breeze, when Joy suddenly noticed that the sky had darkened and the breeze had stiffened considerably. She called to Carole who was ahead, but Carole didn't hear her and continued gliding down the slope toward the boundary of lodge property.

Then, so suddenly that Joy didn't even see how, one minute Carole was skimming along in front of Joy and slightly to her right, and the next moment there was a cracking noise and Carole was sailing through the air. Joy watched in horror as she saw Carole land in a crumpled heap in the snow.

Frantic, Joy moved awkwardly to Carole's side. She saw that one of Carole's skis was broken. Crouching down, she called Carole's name but Carole neither moved nor answered.

As Joy shook Carole's arm and begged her to answer, a series of snowflakes drifted down and landed on Carole's still, white face. A tremor of panic and helplessness ran through Joy's body as she realized that they were in serious trouble!

4

Joy looked up at the sky as a gust of wind, laden with stinging bits of ice and snow, swirled around her. Heavy clouds blotted out all evidence of the sun and the wind was rapidly taking on the force of a gale. Joy stood rooted to the spot and as the gravity of their predicament threatened to overwhelm her, a stronger gust of wind struck her, almost bowling her over. The air filled with large, fluffy snowflakes interlaced with tiny fragments of icy sleet.

Fear pounded in Joy's throat, stupifying her brain. They were a long way from the lodge, and Joy wasn't even sure she knew the way back! Intent on following Carole, she had paid little attention to the way they had come.

Drawing in a frightened, shaky breath, Joy prayed in desperation, "Dear God, please help us!"

Shifting her stricken eyes to the lifeless

form of her friend, Joy prayed the same petition again and was surprised to feel a steadying of her nerves. She bent over Carole, called her name and shook her, none too gently. Intense relief flooded her as she heard a faint sound. Carole moved slightly — as if in slow-motion — and then struggled to sit up while shielding herself from the snowflakes peppering her face.

Joy brushed away the snow clinging to Carole's ashy face and breathlessly asked, "Are you okay?"

"Wha-what happened?" Carole asked, dazedly.

"Your ski must have hit a stump or rock hidden in the snow."

"From the way it feels, I must have hit the rock with my head, too," Carole said, rubbing the left side of her head with a mittened hand. She groaned suddenly and her face twisted in a grimace of pain.

"Let me see," Joy said, and pushed back the parka from Carole's head. Through the wealth of jet-black hair, she saw that blood was seeping from a large bump. Joy pulled off her mittens and found some tissues in a pocket of her ski pants.

"You've got a big bump on your head," Joy said as she made a thick pad of the tissues, wrapped them around some packed

41

snow and placed it over the lump. "That's about all we can do for it 'til we get back to the lodge." Carole held it there while Joy gently pulled the edges of the parka's hood back around Carole's white face and tied the cord.

"Now," Joy tried to speak briskly, "Let's see if we can get you on your feet. This snow is getting heavier by the minute and we need to get home."

"One of my skis is broken!" Carole cried in dismay.

"I know, but it can still be used, I think, at least to help you balance yourself."

Taking Carole's hands, Joy tugged gently. Carole started to rise and then fell back on the snow with an agonized cry.

"My knee! I can't stand! Something is wrong with my knee!"

Joy knelt beside her and asked anxiously, "You're sure you can't put your weight on it?"

"I-I'll try again. Help me."

Gently Joy tried to ease Carole to a standing position but the instant Carole moved her right leg, an agonized cry escaped her. She sank to the ground, her face distorted with pain.

"I've wrenched my knee or s-something," she gasped. "I hope I haven't broken a bone. It hurts dreadfully." Suddenly the seriousness of their situation registered on her face. The blue-black eyes that turned to Joy were wide with fright. "I can't stand, let alone ski, and we're miles from the lodge. What are we going to do?"

Before Joy could form an answer, Carole spoke again. "I'm so sorry, Joy! It was my curiosity that got us into this."

"It doesn't matter who's to blame, Carole; we've just got to get you back to the lodge. Do you suppose you could stand, if you lean on me?"

"It wouldn't work while we are on skis, and without them, it would take forever to cover those miles back to the lodge. You'll just have to go back and get help. It's the only way!"

Joy studied her friend's pale face. She hated to admit that she had no idea how to get back to the lodge. They had climbed hills, skimmed down slopes, crossed dips and wandered through both wooded and open ground. She had never felt any more helpless, useless or fearful in her life.

Carole's eyes locked with Joy's. "You don't know how to get back." Carole stated the fact.

Joy nodded miserably. "I just followed you blindly."

Not wanting Carole to see the terror and panic that was threatening to overwhelm her again, Joy turned her eyes away from her friend's gaze, past the row of flags, across to the far slope. Vaguely, through the falling snow, she saw a patch of dark-red roof, just discernible through the forest!

"There's a house over there! See!"

Carole turned eager eyes in the direction Joy was pointing. "It is a house," she said slowly, "but I'm afraid we won't be very welcome there."

Comprehension dawned in Joy's eyes and a chill swept through her. "Windthorn?"

"Windthorn," reiterated Carole.

Joy tried to speak calmly so Carole would not know how very frightened she was. "Welcome or not, I'll go and get some help for you. Even Skye Windthorn couldn't refuse to help in a situation like this."

But the brave words held a tremor. In her mind's eye, Joy saw a huge brindle dog hurtling toward them and the stern face of Skye Windthorn. But whatever that forbidding house held, she had to go. There was no choice. The storm was growing worse by the minute.

Carole's eyes were troubled when Joy

44

cast a furtive look at her.

"Will you be all right until I get back?" Joy spoke more loudly than necessary to hide her fear. "Are you in pain?"

"The pain's bearable unless I move my leg, but the least movement sets it to throbbing so badly it makes me nauseous," Carole admitted. "But I'll be okay until you get back. And you will be careful of the dog, won't you? If he comes at you, yell your head off. He seems to stick pretty close to his master."

I think I'm as afraid of his master — almost, anyway — as I am of the dog, Joy thought, but she didn't voice her thoughts. Carole needn't know what a coward she was.

As she turned to push off, Carole said softly, "I'll be praying."

"Thanks," Joy said. She started out on her skis, awkwardly at first but gaining confidence as she carefully worked her way down the slope toward Windthorn. Trying not to think of the sleek, savage monster of a dog and his arrogant master, Joy concentrated on her skiing. But her thoughts kept slipping back to what Jeffrey had said of the master of Windthorn.

"He's a strange man. I even wonder if he might be dangerous." A cold chill of fear

45

crept down her back.

"Joy," she scolded herself aloud, "You're scaring yourself needlessly. You have prayed and Carole is praying. Why don't you show a little trust in God?" She managed a little laugh at her fears, and trudged on.

The wind caught at her with renewed force as she reached the bottom of the slope. She stopped to get her bearings. Up a long slope and through the trees, she could now see the faint outline of a huge, blackish-grey stone building. She lingered only a moment and then attacked the slope.

She was completely winded by the time she reached the crest of the hill, but she rested only briefly before crossing a wide expanse of park-like, timbered ground. She came out into a large graveled driveway which circled around in front of the house and disappeared back the way it had begun.

The house was monstrously large and built from blocks of almost black stone. It loomed, bleak and forbidding, over Joy. She removed her skis with slightly unsteady hands, leaning them against a tree before stepping into the snow-packed drive. Taking a deep breath, she threw back her shoulders and faced the house. Her chest felt like a steel band was tightening around it. But the gulps of chilled air helped. She walked quickly and as silently as possible toward the door.

She felt pounding in her ears and knew it was her heart beating a frightened tattoo on her ribs. Almost to the front entrance, she drew a slight sigh of relief. So far she had not seen a living soul — or the Great Dane either.

Joy put her foot on the first of the six deep steps leading up to the cupolaed entrance. Then she saw him! The monstrous animal was standing on the porch. Every inch of him was tensed to spring, and he appeared even bigger, darker, and more savage than he had the other day.

She heard the deep rumble of warning and saw the white gleam of his teeth as the lips drew back in a hideous grimace. Then the Great Dane charged down the steps toward her with a fierce snarl.

In her terror, Joy forgot everything except the monster charging down upon her. With a piercing scream, she turned to flee. Her feet were fleet upon the graveled drive, but the snow and ice patches were treacherous. She hadn't gone twenty feet before she slipped and fell.

Horror and despair washed over her in sickening waves as she struggled to rise and realized the huge dog was almost upon her. Flinging her arms up to protect her face, she drew herself into a ball and tensed for the worst. Almost immediately she felt the hot breath of the animal on her face.

5

Joy drew her head in tighter to her chest and tried to shield her face and throat with her arms. As frightened as she was, oddly, her mind was keenly alert.

The animal was growling savagely. Joy heard the snap of his sharp teeth and waited for the fangs to rip into her flesh. For a long moment she held her breath — but nothing happened. The vicious animal still stood over her, she could feel his hot breath and hear his snarls, but he did no more.

Joy dared not move. Almost paralyzed by fear, she stayed very still, hoping help would come before the dog decided to rip into her body.

Suddenly Joy heard a door slam and running footsteps. She still did not dare to move. The heavy footsteps came swiftly toward her and then she heard a voice heavily laden with sarcasm.

"Well, Prince, where did you get this little snow bunny?"

Joy more sensed than saw the dog draw away from her. Cautiously and carefully, she uncurled herself and sat up. Through the sifting snow, she saw the lean, sardonic face of Skye Windthorn. Close beside him stood the dog, no longer growling but still alertly watching her every move. The man made no effort to help her when she scrambled to her feet on the slippery driveway. He simply stood glaring at her with cold grey eyes.

For a second, anger flared white-hot in Joy's breast. His dog could have torn her into pieces and the man didn't even ask if she was hurt!

Then abruptly Joy remembered her purpose for being here and her anger vanished.

"I'm sorry to trespass on your property again," Joy spoke urgently. "But my friend is lying over there on the mountainside with a badly hurt knee and we're a long way from the lodge."

"I thought I recognized you." Skye regarded her with undisguised dislike glinting in his eyes. "Why were you two trespassing on my property again?"

"We weren't," Joy denied hastily. "Jeffrey

told us where the line was and we were careful to stay on the other side. But please," Joy felt panic beginning to build inside of her again. Was this arrogant man refusing to help them? "We need your help. The storm is getting worse and. . . ."

As if to emphasize her point, a sudden vicious gust of bitterly cold wind swept around them, cutting off her words and almost obliterating Skye for a moment with a whirling blanket of icy snow. Skye said something but the wind whipped the words away.

Without warning, Skye reached out and grasped Joy's arm, propelling her swiftly toward the house. It was all she could do to keep her balance on the slippery driveway with the man's strong hand moving her swiftly along. The wind tore at her and the soft, almost suffocating snowflakes choked and blinded her.

When they reached the porch, Skye freed her arm, opened the heavy door and pushed her inside. It was a relief to be in out of the storm, but Joy was breathless from the headlong dash for the house and from her fear of the strange, bitter man.

And it was cold. Even though they stood inside the darkened entry hall of the mansion, it was almost as bitter inside as it was out of doors.

But Joy didn't have long to ponder on the lack of heat and single small bulb that strove valiantly, but in vain, to light the large hall. Skye turned away and shouted, "Kim!"

Almost instantly, a black-haired, brown-skinned, lithe form, dressed in dark trousers and white shirt, materialized out of the shadows at the end of the hall.

"Yes, boss?" The young man's voice was soft, with an Oriental accent.

"There's a girl over on the hill with a hurt leg. If we don't get her quick, we may not get her at all. This storm is making into a blizzard. Get into some snow gear and meet us in the garage."

"Right, boss." With a flash of white teeth, the young man dashed away.

Fear's icy fingers gathered about Joy's throat and prickled her scalp. If Skye was alarmed about Carole's plight, Joy knew there was reason to fear!

Skye swung back to her and spoke tersely, "Come with me." He took off down the darkened hall with such long strides that Joy had to trot to keep up.

Abruptly aware of soft footsteps behind them, she glanced back over her shoulder. The Great Dane was padding along behind like a dark, silent shadow. Joy's heart missed a beat. For a moment, she had forgotten all about the creature. Now she wondered why the huge animal had not slashed her to pieces with his powerful jaws and sharp fangs.

Summoning her courage, Joy caught up with the rapidly moving Skye and asked, "If you hadn't come when you did, would your dog have — have hurt me?"

Skye's laugh was a short, derisive snort. "He's not trained to kill, only to capture. But he *would* do whatever necessary to keep his captive on the ground until I arrived. He's extremely well-trained."

Joy shuddered. Now she knew why the animal had not harmed her, but the knowledge didn't do much to allay her fears. Both the animal and his master gave her cold shivers and she would be glad when she and Carole were safely back at the lodge, away from Windthorn and its strange occupants.

They turned into another, shorter hallway and then into another which led into the garage — all as cold as the North Pole. As they emerged from the dark hall into the brightly lighted garage, Joy saw a tall, well built man whom she judged to be in his mid-fifties with very black skin and a closely-clipped black beard, attaching a bobsled behind a large snowmobile.

"I see you anticipated our next move, Washington," Skye said appreciatively. "You did well. Time is extremely important."

Glancing up, the man spoke respectfully, "Thank you, sir. Do you want me to go along?"

Skye considered. "Perhaps you should. And we'll take Prince. If we have trouble finding our way back, he can lead us."

Kim, attired in a rough warm mackinaw and heavy boots, rushed out, snapping on a woolly cap as he came.

"You ride behind me," Skye commanded Joy as he mounted the snowmobile with the trailing bobsled. Joy quickly obeyed.

With some of her anxiety eased, her thoughts jumped ahead to where Carole lay unprotected and helpless on the hillside. *Dear Father, please let us get to her in time.* Even in the security of the garage walls, Joy could hear the howl of the wind which seemed to be increasing in volume by the minute.

"Let's go, Prince." At his master's command, Prince sprang nimbly onto the bobsled and stretched out. The other two men climbed on the other machine with Washington steering.

The two machines roared to life with a

touch of the starters. When the garage door slid open, Joy was horrified to see that in the brief time they had been inside, the storm had developed into a full-blown blizzard. Joy had explained as fully as she could recall where Carole was lying before they went out into the storm. But now, as she looked at the curtain of swirling, choking snow obliterating all but vague shadows of trees, dismay and fear congealed into a hard lump in her stomach.

"How will we ever find Carole?" Joy exclaimed fearfully.

"We have a compass. We'll find her, miss," Washington said kindly. His words eased her apprehension. Somehow, even though Skye and Washington looked formidable, there was something about them that inspired confidence. If it were humanly possible, Joy knew these men would bring Carole in safely.

The two snowmobiles were linked together with a heavy chain. As the machines eased out the door, the wind caught and rocked them. Slowly they snaked out into the world of white with Washington and Kim in the lead

Joy crouched down behind Skye and clung to his heavy coat with both mittened hands as the snowmobiles fought their way through the heavily falling snow. The wind shrieked about them as if it were a living monster, grabbing at their clothing and stinging their faces.

It seemed an eternity before they even reached the bottom of the slope and started upward. They slithered and lurched their way slowly up the slope, the whine of the laboring motors in their ears. Joy clung tenaciously to the tall figure in front of her and wondered if the machines could take the pounding.

Desperately afraid, Joy could form only a wordless prayer, but suddenly words from the Bible leaped into her mind.

I will never leave you or forsake you. I am with you always.

Thank you, Father, Joy said in her heart, relaxing against the calm assurance that God was in control.

"There's the line of flags," Skye shouted a moment later. "We should be close to her now!"

They cruised slowly and carefully up the line of flags for several minutes and then down again without any results. They had moved above the line of flags a second time when they heard a faint call. Skye shouted and they heard Carole answer. In a couple of minutes, they saw her.

She was standing on one ski, using the broken one for a crutch, waving at them. As they stopped, Joy scrambled from the snowmobile and ran to Carole, a lump in her throat. She knew it must have caused Carole agony to stand and keep standing under the onslaught of wind and snow so they could locate her.

Carole's face was a bleached grey, but she managed to grin weakly as they reached her. "Thank God you've come," she said.

Washington and Skye carried Carole to the bobsled and Skye quickly removed her remaining ski. Placing the skis beside Carole, the men lashed her to the sled.

When they were ready to go, Prince jumped on the end of the sled, and the snowmobile caravan went slipping and lurching back down the hill.

Almost as if it were backing off for another run, the wind and snow seemed to slack off somewhat and the return trip was accomplished much more quickly. But just as they eased into the long, circular driveway, the wind bore down upon them again with renewed force, as though sensing that its victims were escaping. The enveloping white curtain of snow blotted out everything.

The drivers inched their way along the

length of the drive toward the house. Prince, at a sharp command from his master, jumped from the sled and charged away, barking loudly. The snowmobiles followed slowly and soon found the door of the garage.

The dark grey walls of the windswept mansion seemed almost friendly to Joy. Any sanctuary from the violence of the blizzard was welcome now.

6

Joy followed the men through the house. As soon as they deposited Carole on a bed in a room on the second floor, Skye said brusquely, "Washington will take care of you." Immediately, he turned on his heel and left the room.

Joy stared after him for a long moment then glanced at Carole. Her face was ashen with pain, and perspiration stood out in beads on her forehead. The jostling trip through the house to this room had obviously left her knee and head throbbing almost unbearably.

Washington's dark face mirrored sympathy and concern. He removed Carole's ski boots. "Could you ease off her outer clothes while I'm gone and cover her with this heavy blanket?" he asked Joy.

At her quick nod, he turned to Carole who lay with pale face and tightly clenched hands on the bed. "Now, just lie very still, little lady, and we'll get you more comfortable real soon," he directed. "I'll be right back."

Carole managed a small smile and a faint, "Thank you," closing her eyes as he left the room.

Joy unzipped Carole's parka and gently tugged her out of it. The dark hair was damp from pain-induced perspiration as well as melted snow. Removing the ski pants, even as gently as possible, brought gasps of agony from Carole. Joy was horrified to see that Carole's knee was extremely swollen and bruised.

Quickly covering her with the heavy blanket against the chill of the room, Joy spoke soothingly, "You're going to be all right. Washington seems to be very capable. And I'll stay right here." Carole reached out a slim hand and Joy quickly enclosed it in her own warm hand.

In minutes, Washington was back with Kim. Kim went quickly to the fireplace and began building a fire while Washington set the tray he was carrying on the bedside table. Measuring out a spoonful of liquid from a small bottle on the tray, he dumped it into a glass, then added a little water from a pitcher. "Raise her head a bit," he instructed Joy.

When she did, he placed the glass to Carole's lips. "Drink this," he instructed. "It will ease the pain and make you sleep."

Carole complied and then sank back upon the pillow as if the effort had exhausted her.

Turning to Joy, Washington said, "She should feel better in a few minutes."

Carole cried out once when Washington first moved her knee and then clamped her teeth together and uttered not another word as he gently wrapped her knee in an elastic bandage, elevated it with a fat pillow, and applied an ice-pack. Then he tucked the blanket back around her.

When Washington finished his ministrations, he instructed Joy, "I want her to drink some of that hot soup and some hot tea before she goes to sleep." He smiled kindly, "And I think you should drink a cup of that tea yourself. You look like you need it."

"Thank you," Joy said gratefully, "I believe I will. And thank you so much — for everything."

"It's my pleasure, miss," Washington assured her, his dark eyes crinkling at the corners. "If you need anything, press that buzzer." He showed her where it was and left, promising to check on his patient in a short while. With a quick nod and a reserved smile, Kim followed Washington out the door.

At least Skye's help is kind and hospitable, Joy thought. A surge of anger rose in her. The lordly Skye hadn't even bothered to ask how Carole was feeling or how serious her injury was. *But I guess,* she speculated, *we are fortunate he condescended to rescue us at all, hateful man that he is!*

And, at least we are out of the storm, she mused. *I should be thankful to God . . . and to Skye,* she admitted to herself reluctantly. *If he hadn't helped us, we wouldn't have survived very long out in that blizzard.* Her anger fizzled and died. *I really am grateful,* she thought, *but something about that man makes me so angry. His arrogance, his rudeness, his insolence! From the way he acts, I wonder if he is a misogynist and the very sight of a woman brings out the worst in him.*

She pondered that thought for a minute, and realized that they would probably see little of him while at Windthorn. He seemed grimly reclusive to the point of being unfriendly. Joy shivered involuntarily as an image of Skye Windthorn rose in her mind. Joy felt Carole's hand release hers. Her eyes were closed and shadowed with dark smudges of pain and fatigue. Her face was still deathly white, but her breathing had assumed a more regular, even cadence.

The fire was crackling cheerfully, sending its welcome warmth into the chilly room. Joy rose and poured herself a steaming cup of tea. Carrying the cup, she crossed the room and pushed back the heavy drape to look out. The snow was falling so heavily that she could see only one large branch of a tree breaking the wall of white outside the window and just brushing the glass. Joy shuddered. How thankful she was that they were out of the blizzard! She dropped the curtain and went to stand in front of the fire. Sipping the soothing hot tea, she stared moodily into the snapping, dancing firelight.

Suddenly Carole spoke from the bed, "Joy? Are you here?"

Joy hurried back to her side. "Yes. I thought you were asleep! Is the pain easing?" she inquired

Carole's voice sounded stronger and her dark eyes were open. "Yes, it's already much better. But I'm terribly sleepy. That must have been a powerful drug."

Carole tried to raise up but winced and settled back. "Joy, we must get word to David where we are and that we are safe.

He'll be absolutely frantic by now. Is there a telephone here?"

"Right by your bed," Joy said. "Why don't you lie still and I'll call. And then you had better have some of this hot soup and tea before you go to sleep."

"Thanks."

Joy dialed the number and asked the girl at the front desk of the resort who answered to connect her with David Loring's room.

"Is this Mrs. Loring?" the receptionist asked, excitement ringing in her voice.

"No, this is her friend, Joy Kyle. We. . . ."

The girl on the other end of the line broke in, "Mr. Loring is right here with Mr. Pitman. I'll call him."

Almost instantly David was on the line. His voice sounded distraught. "Joy, what happened to you two? We have been combing the ski slopes and everywhere, searching for you. I've been about to go out of my mind with this storm and all. Is Carole with you? Where are you?"

Joy spoke reassuringly. "Carole is here at Windthorn with me. Carole's ski hit a rock and has apparently wrenched her knee quite badly, but she's going to be fine."

"At Windthorn?" David's voice was

64

grim. "Are you sure you'll be okay there?"

"At the moment we have no choice but to stay here," Joy said, "but we're being treated quite well. Mr. Windthorn helped rescue us so I'm sure he won't harm us." Goosebumps prickled on her arms as she tried to reassure David.

"As soon as the storm slacks up and we can get through, Jeffrey and I will come to get you two," David said emphatically.

"Let me speak to David," Carole broke in. Joy handed the phone to Carole. "David," Carole said, making a valiant effort to speak in a strong, cheerful voice. "We're fine so don't you worry about us."

"Are you in a lot of pain?"

"Some, but it's getting better and better. Skye's butler, or whatever he is, seems to be whiz of a nurse. He gave me something to ease the pain and make me sleep."

When she gave the phone back to Joy a couple of minutes later, Joy saw that Carole could scarcely keep her eyes open. She insisted that Carole drink some of the soup immediately. Carole did manage to take a few sips, but when Joy set the cup of soup down and took up the cup of tea, Carole's head fell back limply against Joy's arm. Joy tried to rouse her to drink a little more of the soup or tea, but Carole could not be awakened.

Slightly alarmed, Joy wondered if it had been necessary to knock Carole out so completely. *Could there be more to it?* Joy moved away from the heavily sedated form of her friend to the window. Even through the thick stone walls of the mansion, she could hear the howling of the wind. Outside the window the frigid, swirling white curtain still enclosed them like an impenetrable wall. Unwillingly, Jeffrey's words about Skye filled her mind. "He's a strange man. I even wonder if he might be dangerous."

Staring rigidly into the night, Joy suddenly realized that she and Carole were alone in this desolate mansion with complete strangers. One was as sinister as the villain in a gothic thriller — and Carole was unconscious. Swiftly Joy crossed the carpeted floor and locked the door.

7

Joy was prowling around the room like a caged cougar a few minutes later when a sharp knock came at the door. Kim, a small smile showing white, even teeth, stood there when Joy cautiously opened the door.

"Mr. Windthorn desires to know if Mrs. Loring is resting well now?"

Well, Joy thought sarcastically, *maybe the master of the house has remembered his manners at last.* But keeping her voice pleasant, she said to the houseboy, "You can tell him that Mrs. Loring is sleeping."

"That is good," Kim said in his soft, pleasantly accented voice. "Mr. Windthorn will be pleased. Also, Mr. Windthorn requests your presence at dinner."

Before Joy could form an answer to this astonishing request, Kim waved a hand toward a door to Joy's left. "The guest room through that door is yours, ma'am. There is a bathroom between it and Mrs. Loring's room. I think you will find everything you need to freshen up for dinner but if you need anything, just press the button and I'll get it for you. Dinner is at five."

With a slight bow, Kim withdrew.

Joy's heart was pounding and her mind was reeling. The arrogant Skye Windthorn had invited her to have dinner with him! Maybe he wasn't a woman hater after all — or maybe he was and he simply wanted to toy with her through his barbed insults.

I really shouldn't go, she thought. *I'm exhausted and just don't feel like being baited and insulted. I could plead tiredness — it would be the truth — and ask for a tray to be brought up.*

But in spite of the fact that she dreaded sharing a meal with Skye Windthorn, she was also intrigued with the idea. She was not only curious to know why he had invited her, there was also an aura of the mysterious and ominous about him that both repelled and drew her.

After checking to see that Carole was still asleep, Joy looked at her watch. She had about thirty minutes before dinner. *Enough for a quick examination of the other bedroom. And even though I don't have any other clothes, maybe I can freshen up a bit.*

Joy quickly passed through the bathroom and opened the other guest room door. An involuntary gasp of surprise escaped her.

The room was done in pink, white, and silver. The wallpaper was a pale pink sparsely sprinkled with little silver bells; the luxurious shag rug and filmy curtains were pure white, and the canopied bed was a silvery-white framed in cotton-soft pink. The room was fit for a princess! It didn't seem to belong with the dark paneling and heavy mahogany furnishings she had seen elsewhere in the austere Windthorn mansion.

Who could this beautiful, feminine room belong to? she wondered. Her eyes widened as a thought came to her. Surely not Skye Windthorn's dead wife! If she had been killed running away with Skye's friend, would he keep her room just as she had left it? If he had, she could only surmise that he had loved her very much. It was a curious thought that the forbidding Skye Windthorn might have loved anyone that much.

Joy crossed the room and rolled back the sliding door of a large closet. She drew in a sharp breath. The closet was filled with beautiful, expensive dresses, long evening gowns, suits, blouses, sweaters, and slacks.

The scent of an expensive perfume filled Joy's senses. Suddenly feeling she was prying into things that didn't concern her, Joy quickly closed the sliding door.

Could those clothes have been Mrs. Windthorn's? How strange for a man to keep his wife's clothing after she had been dead for three years. Then the thought came that perhaps Skye had a girlfriend who visited frequently.

"It's really none of your business, Joy," she told herself aloud sternly. "If they belong to his deceased wife or to a live girlfriend, you aren't responsible to God for anyone's morals but your own."

Joy took one last appreciative look at the frilly pink and white bedroom before retracing her steps to the bathroom. This was also beautifully decorated and luxurious. Although she had no clean clothes to change into, Joy took a quick shower and felt much better. Feeling somewhat like she was dressing for battle, she brushed her hair until it shone like spun-gold and her scalp felt tingly. She even applied a little perfume from the wide assortment of bottles on the dressing table. A few minutes later, when Washington came to inquire about Carole and to bring Joy down to dinner, she was ready.

8

The hall that Washington led her down was chilly and poorly lighted. The question crossed Joy's mind, *Is Skye Windthorn too stingy to light and heat his house?* Then another thought occurred to her. Perhaps he didn't have the money and was being economical. Jeffrey had said that Skye would never have sold him the land for the resort if he hadn't needed money badly. Perhaps he didn't do well professionally or had made poor investments. She knew it must cost a lot of money just to keep a house the size of this one in repairs and to pay the taxes.

Joy had little time to ponder all of this, though, for a moment later Washington drew open double doors and stood back for Joy to enter the dining room. Her heart quickened as she stepped into the room. Her first impression was of warmth, sparkling chandeliers, glowing candles, richly upholstered chairs, and warm, polished wood in furniture and walls. A round table, complete with lace tablecloth, gleaming silver and fine old china, was set a comfortable distance from a huge fireplace where a log crackled cozily.

Skye's huge Great Dane was stretched out near the fireplace. When Joy entered the room, he raised his head and made a move to rise.

Skye, who was standing in front of the fire with his back to her, spoke one low word and the dog settled back down. But Joy felt the dog's eyes fixed upon her as Skye turned toward her, a slight smile on his saturnine face.

He was dressed rather casually in dark trousers and a sweater over a lighter shirt and tie, but he looked so much more formally dressed than she, that Joy heard herself apologizing for her inability to dress for dinner. She was suddenly uneasy and wished she had stayed in her room.

Amusement gleamed in Skye's eyes and his first words did not set her any more at ease. "I thought you might be lonely on such a ghastly night with your friend sound asleep. It isn't often I have the pleasure of a lovely young lady's company, so I decided to make the occasion a gala affair."

There was a mocking light in Skye's dark eyes as he pulled out Joy's chair before taking his own place.

Joy thanked Skye again for rescuing them and apologized for their intrusion.

Skye brushed off her thanks lightly. "I'm glad Mrs. Loring is resting well. And I hope you like my choice of wine," Skye said as he lifted a frosty bottle from its bed of chipped ice.

"Thank you, but no wine for me," Joy said.

Skye's eyebrow shot up, "I can have Washington mix you something else, if you don't care for wine."

"No, thank you; some iced tea or coffee would be fine," Joy said firmly.

But Skye didn't let it rest. "I'm not trying to get you drunk, so you can feel free to have a drink," he said dryly.

Joy wished again that she had stayed in her room but she tried to answer graciously. "I hope you won't be offended, but I just don't drink alcohol of any kind."

Skye's eyes widened in astonishment, "A blonde that doesn't drink! That's a new one!"

Joy felt her face grow warm under his mocking eyes. She felt he was watching her as if she were one of his ancient parch-

73

ments written over with strange symbols and didn't know what to make of her.

Washington returned just then to Joy's great relief, and began serving a soup with a delicious aroma. In spite of her disconcerting dinner companion, Joy suddenly realized she was ravenously hungry.

Lifting a silver soup spoon, Joy tasted the broth. It was as delicious as it smelled. Trying not to wolf it down, Joy kept her eyes on her bowl while she savored two or three more spoonsful. Then glancing up, she saw Skye's amused eyes upon her and almost choked. Somehow a single word or glance from him turned her into an awkward dolt!

Recovering with as much dignity as she could manage, Joy said the first thing that came to her mind. "Did the lovely pink and white room Washington put me in belong to your wife?"

The eyes staring into hers lost their amused look and darkened. Anger glinted there and frosted his words. "Don't ever mention that woman in my presence again!"

Joy dropped her eyes in confusion and dismay. Suddenly she was angry. How dare this arrogant male treat her like a child! Rage wiped out her awe and intimidation.

She laid her spoon down and rose to her feet. Lifting her chin, she looked him squarely in the eyes and spoke with calm dignity. "I'm sorry. I seem to have upset you. Perhaps it would be better if I go back to my room."

She turned and walked quickly toward the door.

"Wait!"

Joy paused. Her first impulse was to stalk on out of the room but inbred courtesy held her. Turning back, she saw that Skye had risen. For a brief instant, Joy saw a raw, unnamed feeling mirrored in Skye's face before the old sardonic mask slipped back in place.

The fleeting emotion was hard for Joy to put a tag on. Sadness — regret — hurt — loneliness? It was hard to say. But for that infinitesimal moment, she thought she glimpsed the lost and lonely man that was Skye Windthorn.

However, when he spoke again, casually but persuasively, the old arrogance was back. "Don't go. I apologize for my rudeness," Skye said, his expression belying his words. "Perhaps I was taking out my animosity on you. You see, two blondes were at one time the special persons in my life, and they both did their best to ruin my life." Bitterness had crept into his voice.

Joy moved almost unconsciously until she stood facing Skye across the table. "People can only do to us what we allow them to do," she said gently.

Anger lanced across Skye's face. "That's easy for you to say! You never loved a mother who was never a mother! And my wife was just like her!" Skye gritted his teeth in fury. "She was a featherbrained manchaser who ran off with my best friend!"

Suddenly aware of how much he was revealing, he sneered, "But I'm sure the gossips have already informed you of all this." His voice rose, high and mimicking, " 'The Windthorns were all perfect idiots when it came to choosing women!' That's the general consensus — and I suppose it's pretty accurate!"

Skye's tirade was tying Joy's stomach into knots. She wished she could escape to her room, but felt it might seem melodramatic to do so now. She tore her eyes from Skye's face and slid back into her chair.

Heaving a sigh, Skye followed her example. "Believe it or not, I really didn't plan to entertain you with my woes. But I didn't feel like a sermon from a sheltered, pampered blonde who knows nothing about the real world!"

Joy's head came up and blue fire flashed from her eyes. Her sarcasm matched Skye's. "You poor mistreated boy! You aren't the only person who's had troubles!"

As she saw fury flare again in his face, she wished she had kept her mouth shut, but she couldn't seem to stop. "Sheltered? Pampered? My father was a tyrant who broke my mother's heart and health. When I left home at the age of seventeen to live on my own, he disowned me. And my husband was even worse! He ran out on me as soon as he knew I was pregnant, and for five years I lived in fear that he would come back — until he was killed by. . . ."

Joy suddenly shuddered and shut off the rash flow of words. She never ranted like that, and to spill out her whole life's history to a perfect stranger was mortifying. She stole a glance at Skye.

Shock and incredulity were written on his countenance.

"You're not putting me on?" he finally said.

Joy shook her head. Her rage was gone. "But things are fine now. My father and I were reconciled to each other recently and . . ."

"The soup is cold so I think I had better call for Washington to bring the next course," Skye broke in, "unless you would like him to reheat the soup."

"No, the next course is fine," Joy said, surprised at the brusque tone in his voice.

In response to his ring, Washington came almost instantly, as if he had been hovering just out of sight awaiting the summons.

When baked ham, salad, yams and other vegetables were on the table, Washington again withdrew. Skye sliced the ham and served their plates.

After Joy had taken a few bites and praised everything, Skye abruptly returned to their previous conversation. "You said you and your tyrant father got back together?" he said, seemingly genuinely interested.

"Yes, Dad met a young couple — Carole Loring, my friend upstairs, and her husband, David. I won't go into the whole long story, but through them my father became acquainted with God and just recently accepted Christ as his Savior. Naturally the next step was to bring me back home." Joy's voice was soft with emotion. "Even after six months it still doesn't seem possible."

Skye said nothing for a long moment. When he spoke, he ignored her reference to God. "What did you do for a living after your father disowned you?"

"My mother had saved some money for the time she felt I would have to make a life on my own. I trained to work with computers and have been able to manage fine. When Mitzi was born . . ."

"A daughter."

"Yes, a five-year-old daughter who is the joy of my life."

Skye studied Joy's face. When she spoke of her child, her blue eyes and expressive face glowed. Her mere prettiness became a certain radiance that made her beautiful.

Joy was suddenly uncomfortably aware of Skye's close scrutiny and said the first thing that came to mind, "I understand your little son was killed in a plane crash. I'm sorry."

Skye's eyes went bleak. "The gossips have informed you well, I see."

Joy felt the hot wave of color rise in her face. "Not really, but naturally people are intrigued by a man who lives a rather secluded life."

Wishing to change the subject, Joy went on. "They also say that you are an archaeologist and an expert in ancient writings."

Joy was amazed at the effect of her words. She had unwittingly discovered the topic that Skye lived and breathed. The remainder of the meal he talked with animation and obvious pleasure about archaeology. He had been all over the world and told fascinating stories of his life at different excavations and places in the world.

Joy was astonished that this cynical man could be such a delightful companion. When he spoke of his work, the arrogance dropped away and he became a different person. She found she was reluctant for the meal to end.

"At present I'm working on a very old leather scroll," Skye said as the meal was coming to a close.

"Would it be possible for me to see it?" Joy asked. "I've never seen any ancient writing, not even in a museum."

Skye looked pleased. "Certainly. All I ask is that you don't handle it."

After dessert Skye led Joy through the drawing room into his study. Unlocking a deep drawer in his desk, he removed a thin case. Opening it, he gently drew out a ragged edged object. "This is believed to be a sheet from an account book," he said. "I've just started working on it, though, so I'm not sure yet."

"I imagine it is extremely valuable," Joy said in awe.

"No value can be set on objects of this

kind," Skye said. "They could not be replaced and of course are not for sale. This one belongs to a museum in Egypt."

"Isn't it a terribly big responsibility to have such an irreplaceable object in your home?" Joy asked.

"It's pretty heavy," Skye admitted, "but I always take every precaution possible to insure the safety of anything I'm working on."

Joy shuddered. "Have you heard there have been some burglaries in this area recently?"

Skye smiled. "The Midnight Cat Burglar? Yes, the sheriff keeps me informed. I am concerned somewhat, but I really can't see a burglar who has only taken jewelry and money in the past being interested in an ancient scroll. It would be very difficult to sell."

"Yes, I suppose it would be hard to find a buyer for it," Joy agreed.

"However," Skye said, "I'm taking no chances. I always lock it up when I'm away from it even briefly. And my two men are alert and dependable."

"You have a fascinating line of work," Joy said as Skye locked the scroll back into the desk.

"Yes, it is," Skye said with a faint smile,

"but lots of hard, painstaking work, too. Now, let's get back to the present. Do you play the piano?"

Joy hesitated. "Yes — I do, but I'm really not a talented musician. Carole plays beautifully but I only entertain myself. Do you play?"

"I thought you would never ask," Skye said with an almost boyish grin. "If it wouldn't bore you, I would be happy to bang out a few chords for you."

"A man of many talents," Joy said. "I would love to hear you play."

"I'm no professional but I do enjoy playing. The piano's in the drawing room." He rose and led the way. Prince, totally ignoring Joy, paced behind them with his eyes on Skye's back, as majestic as a king.

A very fine grand piano held the place of honor in the beautifully furnished drawing room next door. Skye asked Joy to play first but she declined. As soon as Skye ran his fingers over the keyboard, Joy knew he was a talented pianist. She was a lover of music and had always lamented that she had no real talent for any instrument. For the next several minutes she sat in rapturous attention and drank in the music that poured from Skye's skillful fingers.

But gradually something began to nibble

at Joy — a nebulous, uneasy feeling. At first she tried to shake it away and lose herself again in the music. Then suddenly she knew what the feeling was! Someone was watching her!

Skye's attention was still totally riveted in the piece of music before him. Joy let her eyes rove furtively about the room. No one else was visible, but prickles of apprehension and alarm ran down Joy's back. She tried to force herself to concentrate on the music, but the feeling that she was being watched by hidden eyes persisted.

Once again Joy let her eyes slide over the room and even turned her head to look behind her. There was no one else in the room. Then out of the corner of her eye she caught a flicker of movement in a long, heavy velvet curtain. Turning her head slightly so she could look without seeming to, she waited.

She was about to decide that she had imagined the movement when the curtain rippled slightly again. She was almost certain that for a brief second an eye and a tuft of blonde hair were visible where the two halves of the curtain met. There was another very faint ripple of the curtain and the eye vanished. Joy thought she detected the sound of furtive footsteps retreating, but she wasn't sure.

Joy jumped as she heard Skye say a trifle crossly, "I've already lost my audience so I must be boring you."

"No — no, it isn't that," Joy stammered. "It's just that I had this feeling that someone was watching me and — and it distracted me."

"Why would anyone be watching you?" Skye scoffed.

"I-I don't know. It was probably just my imagination, but I also thought I saw that curtain over there move," she said, pointing.

Skye rose quickly and strode across the room to draw back the curtain. Behind it was a short, narrow passageway, dimly lighted but very obviously empty.

Skye turned back toward Joy, the mocking light back in his eyes. "As you can see, there is no one there. It is an eerie night. I'm sure your imagination was playing tricks. And I'm also sure you are tired and would like to retire. I'll call Washington to show you to your room."

Staring silently at him in some dismay, Joy felt that she had been dismissed.

Skye pressed a button on the wall and Washington appeared almost instantly. Joy wondered uneasily if he was the one who had been watching her behind the curtain. Then she pushed the thought away as ridiculous.

Joy thanked Skye for a pleasant dinner and the excellent music to which he only inclined his head in acknowledgment and bade her goodnight. His eyes were no longer friendly.

9

When they arrived back at Carole's room, Washington went in with Joy and checked his patient. She was still deep in a relaxed sleep.

"The lady will be much better tomorrow, I'm sure," he said comfortingly. "She should sleep all night, but if she does wake up and is in pain, just ring me and I'll come." Washington then added that she was welcome to use the nightwear and other clothing in her room. "It belonged to Mr. Windthorn's wife and she was about your size."

Joy thanked him for his concern and followed him to the door. Staring briefly at the lock, she made a quick decision and turned the bolt behind him. Then she went into her own sleeping quarters and locked that door. She still was not sure someone hadn't been staring at her from behind the curtain in the drawing room, and the feeling made her uneasy.

Although it was early, Joy decided to go to bed. She was very tired, and her ego felt bruised at Skye's curt dismissal. He no doubt thought she was a neurotic, and she realized that his opinion of her mattered more than she liked to admit.

As Joy crossed the room toward the closet, she stopped suddenly. A large picture of a waterfall in a rain forest setting was crooked. *Strange,* she thought as she straightened it, *I didn't notice that hanging crooked earlier.*

Deciding to explore a little, Joy walked over to a large bureau. Instantly she forgot about the crooked picture. Her heart beat fast with pleasure as she lifted out several exquisitely beautiful long nightgowns from the top drawer. She chose a pink one to wear and found a long, fleecy, rose colored robe in the closet.

She checked on Carole again before she went to bed, and seeing her so soundly asleep felt an unexpected lonely feeling. Scoffing at herself, Joy went to her own room, leaving the door open between the rooms in case Carole woke up and needed her. She left a dim light on in Carole's room, but darkened her own.

Although certain that sleep would be

slow in coming, extreme weariness claimed her. Joy was asleep almost by the time she lay her head on the pillow.

"Mommy!" It was Mitzi's little girl voice calling her from the next room. "Mommy, can I get in your bed? I'm scared."

Joy called back, "Of course you can, honey. Come get in Mommy's bed."

Locked in a dream, she heard Mitzi's little bare feet padding across the room and then felt her warm little body snuggling down beside her. Joy hugged her close.

"Mamma?" Joy stiffened in her dream. That was not Mitzi's voice and Mitzi never called her 'mamma.' Cool, soft fingers touched her face and again she heard the soft, "Mamma?"

Neither the voice nor the touch were those of her daughter!

Suddenly Joy was wide awake. She sat up in bed. The strange voice had been so real! And she could still feel the touch of those cool fingers on her face!

Her wide, frightened eyes stared out into the darkened room. Fear beat in her throat and her heart pounded like surf against a cliff. Was someone in her room?

"Who's there?" Her voice quavered. Was someone there in the darkness, scarcely breathing, just watching her? "Who are you? What do you want?" Her voice was tinged with panic.

She heard a slight rustling and then a door closed with a faint click.

Joy felt as if her heart would reverberate out of her body. She reached a shaking hand out to the lamp on her nightstand and snapped it on. Her eyes swept the room. There was no one there. Could she have imagined it all? Was it part of her dream?

Joy braced herself upright in bed and breathed deeply several times. Her heartbeat slowly returned to normal. Rolling out of bed, she slipped her feet into scuffs and padded into Carole's room. She was still sleeping deeply. Joy searched the closets in both rooms as well as the bathroom before she was satisfied no one was in their quarters. Tiptoeing quietly through Carole's room, she checked the door. It was securely locked

Returning silently to her own room, Joy tried to convince herself it had only been a dream. *It must have been a dream,* she reasoned, *and the strange voice calling "mamma," and the cool fingers touching my face were just a vivid part of that dream.*

She climbed back into bed and started

to settle down under the covers when she suddenly realized that she hadn't checked her own door. Feeling a bit silly, she got out of bed again and without putting on her robe, dashed across the cool room and tried the door.

It opened easily in her hand! She knew she had carefully locked that door before going to bed. Someone *had* been in her room after all!

For a moment Joy was too petrified with shock to move, then she dashed back across the room and grabbed her robe. Shrugging quickly into it, she ran back, opened the door and stepped into the hall. The wail of the storm penetrated like a forsaken banshee even here. Her eyes swept the dimly lit hallway both directions but she saw no one. She stood there, undecided whether to charge down the hall in search of the intruder or to summon Washington.

In the bright light from her room, she looked at the watch on her wrist. It was two minutes past eleven o'clock. *I'll go back in the room and ring for Washington,* she decided. It would be foolhardy to go dashing through the halls. And what would she do if she caught the intruder? As she turned back into her room, though, her ears caught the sound of hushed footsteps down the hall to her right. She waited, scarcely breathing.

Around the bend at the end of the hall swung a tall figure, not moving fast, but walking steadily toward her. Backing up against the bedroom door, she waited. In the dim light she was unable to distinguish who it was. But the figure spoke as it neared her, and she recognized the voice of Washington.

"Is something wrong, miss?" Washington moved into the light from her doorway. His dark, puzzled eyes met hers.

"Someone was in my room just now!" A slight quiver betrayed her fear.

Washington's eyes widened in unbelief. "Surely not. What made you think someone was in your room? Did you see someone?"

Joy took a deep breath to calm herself. "I was dreaming that my little girl called 'Mommy.' She was scared and I told her to get into my bed. In the dream she did, and then I heard another voice say 'Mamma,' and felt cool fingers touch my face. The voice and touch woke me up."

The deeply etched creases around Washington's eyes crinkled into lines of merriment as he chuckled, "Miss Joy, you just thought you were awake, that's all. There was no one there in your room. It was just a dream."

"There was!" Joy said decisively. "I had locked our doors — mine and Carole's — before going to bed. But just now when I checked, Carole's was still locked but mine was unlocked!"

A strange expression flickered across Washington's face, something she couldn't define. His eyes shifted away from her face. She thought his chuckle a little forced.

"You must have just thought you locked your door," he said.

"I'm positive I locked it!"

"This is an old house, Miss Joy, perhaps the lock didn't catch." Washington's patient, plausible words began to shake her certainty that someone had been in her room. But her fright was too real to be dismissed so easily.

"But someone *was* in my room and said 'mamma' and touched my face and nearly scared me to death," Joy said stubbornly.

Washington seemed to be considering her words. "This voice that you thought you heard, was it an adult's voice or a child's voice?"

"It was a child's voice — and I'm almost sure it was a boy's. Is there a child here at Windthorn?"

Washington looked away down the hall to her left and then back. His voice was calm but emphatic. "Miss Joy, I can assure you that no one in this house would harm you or your friend. Perhaps the voice and touch were the simple result of the storm, your natural anxiety about your own child, and being in a strange place." Washington paused before adding with a light chuckle, "Windthorn *can* be a gothic monstrosity at times — especially in a storm like this."

"Perhaps you're right," Joy said grudgingly. "Maybe I did dream the voice and touch. And perhaps the lock did spring open again or didn't really lock. Maybe this big, strange house and the storm is making me paranoid."

Joy heaved a sigh. "Thank you for setting my mind at ease. And please don't tell Sk— Mr. Windthorn that I thought someone was in my room. Tonight in the drawing room I imagined someone was staring at me from behind some curtains and I'm sure he thought I was neurotic. Maybe this weather and the fright of Carole's being hurt *is* getting to me."

But even as Joy almost convinced herself, she glanced back at Washington's face, and saw a guarded, watchful expression. She had the feeling that he was listening closely to her words about thinking someone was watching her. Why? Did he think she was a little crazy? Or could he be intensely interested in the possibility that somebody was spying on her? *Was* it her imagination?

Washington inclined his head in a polite manner, "Goodnight, miss. And don't worry, I won't mention your dream to Mr. Windthorn."

Joy went back into her room thoughtfully. She had been ready to believe the soothing answers Washington gave her but something about Washington bothered her. She had the distinct feeling that he knew more than he was admitting.

Suddenly her pulse quickened. Now that she thought about it, Washington had been evasive when she asked if there was a child here. But if there was, surely there would be no need to hide the fact.

Too numb to sort through it all tonight, Joy decided to go back to bed. Maybe the storm would blow itself out during the night and she and Carole would be back in the bright, cheerfulness of Forest Lakes Lodge tomorrow. The thought was vastly cheering. Just as she pulled the covers up and turned off the light, she thought of Jeffrey Pitman and her heart warmed. The admiration in his hazel brown eyes and his frank preference for her company would be very soothing to her pride after the short time she had spent in ill-tempered, sarcastic Skye Windthorn's presence.

Another thought startled her. Maybe the demeaning sarcasm Skye seemed to specialize in had driven his wife into another man's arms. How despicable! A sudden feeling of pity for the poor girl who had been his wife touched her spirit.

10

When Joy awoke, the darkness had faded to a dull grey. She sprang out of bed, rushed to the window and parted the heavy drapes. The world outside was still obscured by a heavy screen of falling snow. The only thing she could see — the single branch of a huge tree outside her window — was bending and bucking under the onslaught of the savage wind. Joy dropped the drape with a heavy heart. They were still trapped. There was no leaving Windthorn today, it seemed.

As she went to wash her face, Joy marveled that she had gone to sleep so quickly and slept so soundly after her fright of the night before. Then she remembered the prayer she had spoken last night asking God's safety for Carole and herself.

This morning, as she offered praise for His protection, she remembered how God had brought her stubborn, egotistical father to his knees in humble submission and reunited them. No miracle could be greater, she thought. And God had already provided. He could certainly take care of two women at Windthorn.

As Joy emerged from the bathroom, she heard Carole's voice. Her heart quickened at the sound and she moved into the adjoining bedroom.

Carole was sitting up in bed and looking quite refreshed, though there were faint dark smudges beneath her eyes. When she saw Joy, Carole said cheerfully, "I wondered if you planned to sleep all day."

Joy glanced at her watch and was amazed to see that it was nine o'clock. "Say, I almost did! How's your knee?"

"As long as I don't move it, it's fine." Carole grimaced, "Which means I'm stuck here in bed for a bit, it seems."

There was a soft tap on the door. Joy unlocked the door and admitted Kim who asked if they were ready for breakfast to be brought up.

After he had gone, Joy said thoughtfully, "At least Kim and Washington are pleasant and friendly even if the master of Windthorn is not."

"Skye Windthorn is still his obnoxious, sarcastic self, then?"

Joy laughed. "Well, to do him justice, he

hasn't been all that bad. He invited me to eat dinner with him last night."

Carole's dark eyes widened at that and she said teasingly, "La-dee-da!"

"Except for a few unpleasantries right at first, he was quite entertaining and hospitable. But the evening didn't end on a very good note."

"Tell me about it! And by the way, where did you come by that stunning robe you're wearing?"

Carole wasn't content until Joy had related everything that had happened — not only at dinner the night before — but from the minute she had left Carole on the hillside to go for help.

Joy told it all, mostly over the delicious breakfast of buckwheat pancakes, sausage and eggs that Kim returned with in record time.

When Joy had finished her narrative, Carole, her dark eyes mirroring concern, asked, "Now that you've slept on it, do you really think someone was in your room last night?"

Joy considered. "I just don't know. But if that voice and touch didn't really happen, that was the most vivid dream I ever had."

"But if there is a child here at Windthorn, why would anyone try to hide his presence?"

"That's what I asked myself," Joy admitted. "I suppose it was just a nightmare. This old, dark mansion reminds me, as Washington said last night, of the setting for a gothic novel. I may just be letting it get to me."

"Our rooms are warm and cheerful, anyway," Carole said.

"Yes, all the rooms that are really lived in are. But the rest of the house is as cold and gloomy as a morgue. I suppose it costs a fortune to heat a house this large so Skye just heats what is used. I wonder if he is strapped financially? And what lengths he might go to to hold on to the family estate?"

"Maybe he's just naturally frugal," Carole suggested as a knock on the door interrupted them.

Washington came in to see how Carole was faring and offered to give her something for pain but she declined. Her leg throbbed, but as long as she didn't move about, it wasn't too uncomfortable. And the bump on her head had all but disappeared along with her headache.

Thanking Washington for his thoughtfulness and kindness, Carole asked him to convey her thanks to Skye for his hospitality.

"Mr. Windthorn is most concerned about your knee and will be pleased that it is improving. He wants you both to make use of any clothing in the closets and chests of drawers. There's a chess set in the closet there, and the library — at the foot of the stairs — is at your disposal. I can also send up a radio if you'd like."

"Oh, please do," Joy said, "then we can hear the weather news."

Washington walked to the door, then turned back. "You probably will not see much of Mr. Windthorn," he said regretfully. "His work keeps him very busy."

"Is it safe for me to go downstairs to the library by myself?" Joy asked doubtfully. "Because of the dog, I mean?"

Washington smiled, "You have nothing to worry about, miss. Prince understands that you're a guest here now. However, he is usually with Mr. Windthorn."

Washington left, promising to give Carole something that evening to make her sleep if it was needed.

The day passed slowly. Carole tried to call the lodge but discovered to her dismay that the phone lines were down. According to the news on the radio, the storm was the worst to hit the area in a decade, and there was no relief in sight for at least another two or three days and maybe not then. They were truly isolated!

After lunch, Carole decided to take a nap. So Joy went down the curving stairway to the library. To her delight, she found that it contained any type of book either she or Carole could desire, even a couple of Bibles. One was a huge family Bible on a small antique desk. It was obviously very old and Joy could not resist lifting the heavy leather cover and gently turning its yellowed pages.

In the front were pages of family records: births, deaths and marriages. Joy read through the record curiously. Toward the end of the fourth page she found the name Skye Terald Windthorn followed by his birthdate. Then the date of his marriage nine years ago to Lillian Fay Weaver.

Terald Benjamin Windthorn, a son, was born to Lillian and Skye a year later. Beneath the son's birthdate was the date of Terald's mother's death and there the record ended.

For a full moment Joy stared at the last date, the death of Lillian Fay Windthorn as the significance of the record slowly registered. *That's odd,* she thought, *there's no record of the little boy's death.* She turned the page and then the next. Although the next two pages were family record sheets, there were no other entries.

Joy turned back to the perplexing last entry and studied it again. And then realized the truth! Terald Benjamin Windthorn was not dead! If he had been dead, this scrupulously kept record of several generations of Windthorns would have recorded it.

Joy suddenly felt a chill tiptoe down her spine. Had she stumbled onto a carefully guarded secret? She closed the Bible and went quickly to a bookshelf, took out four books at random, picked up the small Bible and hurried back upstairs.

Slipping into her own room quietly, she laid her books down gently, then sank into a small platform rocker. For the moment she wanted to be alone and think about what she had just discovered.

Her mind churned with unanswered questions. She clasped her hands together and found that they were cold and clammy. A big lump seemed to have lodged in the pit of her stomach. What was going on in this strange household?

One thing she now knew. Someone *had* been in her room last night. "Mamma" spoken softly twice had been in the voice of a little boy. Terald Windthorn was still alive and had visited her room last night!

But wasn't it unusual behavior for an eight-year-old to come into a strange woman's room in the middle of the night, touch her face, and call her mamma? Could he have been in the airplane crash and survived — with some kind of mental handicap? Was the child dangerous and Skye unwilling to put his only son in an institution?

Fear's icy finger ran lightly over her every nerve ending. But surely Skye would not allow a dangerous person — even a child — to roam at will throughout the mansion.

But the persistent prickling sensation continued. *What if he was locked away and escaped?* Hadn't she heard that persons with unbalanced minds were sometimes extremely cunning?

Joy shivered as a thought struck her. The child apparently had a key to her room!

11

For a long while Joy sat in the rocker, slowly rocking back and forth. Quietly, she began praying.

"Father, please calm my nerves and show me what to do. Should I tell Carole about my suspicions or will it only upset her? Is there really any danger connected with this little boy? Maybe I'm wrong and there isn't a little boy. Maybe Skye was too grief-stricken to record his son's death. This whole thing may be just a figment of my imagination."

The idea arrested her words. Yes, that was a possibility. Maybe there really wasn't a child. If only there was a way to be sure — one way or the other. It wasn't any of her business, of course, unless the child's presence meant danger for either herself or Carole. Or, if there was a child, she might be able to help him — if Skye would allow it which seemed highly unlikely.

The softly spoken "mamma" haunted her until slowly a plan formed in her mind. She would wait up tonight, with only a dim nightlight on, and see if the child came back. This was Terald's mother's room and there was every possibility that if the little boy was alive, he would pay her another visit. It was a plan worth trying!

Suddenly she was excited and exhilarated. Gone was her fear. After all, if she was awake, there was nothing to fear from an eight-year-old child!

"Thank you, Lord," she whispered, "I'll accept this as your direction for the present."

The remainder of the day questions filled her mind. What would happen tonight? Was Terald really alive? If so, would he return tonight?

That evening as she and Carole were eating the delicious roast beef dinner that Kim had brought up to them, Carole suddenly laid down her fork and looked keenly at her friend. "You're up to something, Joy Kyle! What gives?"

Joy tried to look innocent but Carole grinned wickedly. "Don't play dumb with me! You've looked like the cat that ate the prize canary ever since I woke up from my nap. Come on, tell me what's going on."

Joy felt the color rise in her face and knew she couldn't deceive Carole. "Oh, well, I've been dying to tell you, anyway. I just didn't want to worry you."

So Joy told about her discovery that the date of Terald Windthorn's death was missing from the family record in the old family Bible downstairs and about her plan for the night.

Carole's face registered concern, "I don't know, Joy. If there is a child here and he is mentally deranged, even an eight-year-old might be dangerous. Maybe you should sleep in here with me the rest of the time we're here and forget about being a Sherlock Holmes."

"You're usually the adventurous one and I'm the one who holds back," Joy charged. "Now, who's 'chicken'?"

"I'm accustomed to dashing into things without much thought of the consequences, but I guess it scares me for anyone else to do it," admitted Carole. "But if you're bound and determined to try this plan, just be sure you leave the door open between our rooms and let out a big scream at the least hint of danger. If I can't hobble very fast, I could at least press the buzzer and get some help in a hurry."

Although fearful that Carole would stay

awake and keep the vigil with her, Joy agreed to leave the door open and call for help if it was needed.

But by night time, Carole's knee was throbbing and she was exhausted — apparently not yet recovered from her ordeal — and she fell asleep right after dinner.

Joy dimmed the light in Carole's room and locked the door into the hall. She even set a heavy chair against it. She didn't want a curious, possibly deranged, boy in Carole's room. But she did leave the connecting doors between their rooms open as she had promised.

Back in her own room, Joy turned the bedside light on dim leaving the bed faintly illuminated and the rest of the room in deep shadows. Moving the small platform rocker away from the bed into the shadows, she placed it so she could sit in it without being seen, while still having a clear view of anyone at the bedside.

Then Joy turned on the overhead light and tried to read but she couldn't concentrate. She kept listening for strange sounds, and the old house had plenty of those. Even the thick stone wall could not shut out all the sounds of the blizzard, and there was still sufficient wood throughout the huge building to creak and snap as the building cooled off after the heat was turned down.

At ten o'clock, Joy decided it was late enough to put her plan into action. She turned down the bed and placed pillows in it to form a rough figure of a body, then pulled up the covers as if they nearly covered her face.

Taking off only her shoes, she dimmed the light and curled up in the rocker with a blanket wrapped about her against the chill of the cooling room.

She had found a tiny pencil flashlight in a desk drawer and now used it every few minutes to check the time. The moments dragged slowly by. Her nerves grew taut from straining to hear a key turning in the lock or footsteps outside the door. And her eyes began to sting from peering into the murky darkness whenever she heard a slight sound.

When she checked her watch at six minutes before twelve, Joy was about ready to admit defeat. The night before he had been here by eleven. Surely an eight-year-old would not be roaming about at midnight. Maybe there wasn't a child after all and she was losing her sleep for nothing.

Leaning back in the chair, she yawned and realized that in spite of the strain of watching, she was growing sleepy. "A few more minutes is all I'll give you," she said softly into the darkened room.

But when he came, she almost missed him! She awoke with a start at the sound of a soft, "Mamma." And there standing next to the bed in the faint light was a very small boy, not much taller than her own little five-year-old Mitzi. Dressed in pajamas with feet in them, he was staring fixedly at the bed. He took a step closer and said that one word again, "Mamma."

Joy had not planned what to do if a child did appear. And now she still did not know what to do. If she flashed on a light, no doubt he would bolt before she had a chance to talk to him and suddenly she wanted very much to talk to this strange little boy who wasn't supposed to exist anymore.

Putting her hand on the switch of the lamp sitting on a little table beside the chair — she planned to at least get a good look at this mystery child if he ran — Joy spoke very softly.

"Hi, Terald."

The little figure swung quickly around and in the murky light she could see his eyes, wide and startled. He was poised for flight.

Joy spoke again very softly. "Don't be

afraid, Terald. I want to be your friend."

Terald bolted and ran for the door.

Joy snapped on the light and called softly but urgently, "Don't go, I won't hurt you."

The child paused at the door in his headlong flight and looked back at her. With great effort, she remained seated in the chair and smiled. For a moment blue, blue eyes filled with terror stared at her out of a chalky-white face. The skin of his thin hands — one clutched a tattered, lop-eared brown stuffed dog to his thin chest — were so pale they were almost transparent. Straight, lifeless blond hair hung limply about the thinnest face she had ever seen.

Joy's heart contracted with pity. This was the most pathetic looking child she had ever seen. What had been done to this child? What had put the terror in those beautiful blue eyes?

Joy slowly stretched out her hand, "Please don't be afraid. I won't hurt you. I . . ."

The child fled.

Springing from her chair, Joy ran to the door and looked down the hall to her left. The tiny figure in blue pajamas was racing down the hall as if demons were pursuing him.

Without even thinking, Joy ran after him.

12

By the time Joy reached the door, she saw the child whisk around a corner out of sight. Joy sprinted down the hall but stopped abruptly as she came to the corner. The boy had vanished. She surveyed the passageway before her. In the poor light, she could only vaguely see several doors on either side of the hall.

In her stocking feet, she moved softly along the hall, passing two doors on each side. She saw no lights shining under them and heard no movement or voices anywhere.

Suddenly she realized how far she was from her room and that that beast of a dog might be prowling the halls of Windthorn. At the thought, her mouth went dry and her legs grew weak. Turning around, she moved swiftly back toward her own room.

Passing the last door on her right, she thought she heard a growl but didn't stay to find out. Tossing aside all stealth, she fled around the corner and was almost back to the safety of her room when she heard a call.

"Mrs. Kyle?"

Her heart sank. It was Skye's voice and she certainly didn't feel up to any of his sarcasm tonight. She slowed to a walk and took the few remaining steps to the welcome light of her open doorway before she turned.

Prince paced beside his master as they came up to her. So she *had* heard a growl! The dog had, without a doubt, revealed her presence in the hall to his master.

Feeling somewhat like a child caught with her hand in the cookie jar, Joy took a deep breath before she lifted her eyes to meet the glare of Skye Windthorn. He wasn't smiling but his eyes were more quizzical than angry as they met hers.

"Is there a problem, Mrs. Kyle?"

When she hesitated, he went on, "I had just retired for the night and I thought Prince growled. When he growled the second time about a minute later, I thought perhaps I should investigate. Are you ill or do you need something?"

Squaring her shoulders and drawing a deep breath, Joy said firmly, "A little boy was just in my room. He ran out so I followed him."

A look of incredulity sprang into Skye's eyes, then his lips tightened into a thin line. For a long moment he said nothing. Then with a sigh, he said simply, "My son, Terry."

Joy had expected him to deny the boy's presence, as Washington had evaded it last night. This admission of the boy's existence left her at a complete loss.

"B-but I thought he was killed in the plane crash with his mother."

"I had him flown to a hospital for special treatment and the word spread that he had died. I just let everyone think that he had. Especially when he never got any better."

Skye's eyes mirrored extreme weariness. "I hope the child didn't frighten you. Terry used to go to his mother's room after she died but he seldom leaves his room any more so I never thought he would bother you. I'll see that he doesn't come to your room again."

"It's all right," Joy assured him, relieved that the boy had not been a figment of her imagination. "I wasn't frightened when your son came tonight, but he nearly scared me to death last night. He woke me out of a sound sleep by touching my face and calling me mamma."

Skye's head jerked up and his eyes narrowed. "You must be mistaken. He couldn't have spoken to you!"

"But he did! And he spoke again tonight."

Deep emotion swept over Skye's face. He reached out a hand and gripped Joy's arm until she winced. He relaxed his grip but still held her arm. "That child hasn't spoken since his mother was killed! Think carefully, are you positive he spoke?"

"Just the word 'mamma,' but he said it distinctly both nights."

Abruptly Skye released Joy's arm. "I'm detaining you so I'll say goodnight." Without another word, Skye turned and with Prince beside him, strode away down the hall.

Joy stood and stared after Skye until he and the dog disappeared around the corner without a backward glance.

She was baffled. Skye Windthorn was the strangest man she had ever met. A complete paradox. One never knew how he would act. Most of the time he was surly and rude, arrogant and sarcastic. But about the time one expected that, he would switch and be a charming host or, as he was now, a bewildered, weary father worried about his son.

Joy went slowly back into her room and closed the door. She didn't bother to lock it this time.

And Terald — Terry. What was wrong with him? Was he still grieving over his mother's death? It was not normal for a child as young as Terry was when Lillian Windthorn died in that plane crash to still be grieving. It had been three years. Or was the problem due to an injury — perhaps to his head? Could his problem be psychological?

But he was so thin and undernourished. Had his grief affected his appetite — or was he an abused child? Joy shrank from such a thought. Skye might be morose and obnoxious at times, but he had displayed concern for the child just now. Or was it the man who was a beast — and even dangerous as Jeffrey had hinted — perhaps unhinged mentally and abusive to the child?

She pursued the terrifying thought further. Terry looked nothing like his father with his pale fair skin and blue eyes, so he must resemble his mother. Could Skye hold such a grudge against his wife that he would mistreat — maybe even starve — his son since Lillian was beyond his power to punish?

Preposterous! You are letting your imagination get carried away, she hooted at herself. But her thoughts went back to Terry. The terror in his eyes and his almost emaciated little form, clothed in rumpled blue pajamas, rose into her mind. Her heart constricted with pain and pity. If only she could help him! But he was terrified of her, so what could she do? Was he terrified of his father and the servants, too? She wished she knew.

The lonely howl of the storm, muted by the heavy stone walls, only underlined her concern. She prayed earnestly that the child could be helped some way. And, after a while, she found she was praying for Skye, too. If only he could become acquainted with God and accept Christ as his Savior, his whole outlook on life would be changed. *He frightens me,* she thought, *and I could never talk to him about the Lord,* but she knew there was no one in the world who more needed what God could give than Skye Windthorn!

Sleep was a long time coming to Joy that night. There was another storm raging inside the bleak mansion of Windthorn. And, although unsure of its nature, she knew something was very, very wrong.

13

Joy did not see Skye at all the next day.

She slept in since she had been up so late the night before. While Joy was splashing water on her face in the bathroom, Carole called, "I'm dying to hear what happened last night. Did the mystery boy put in his appearance?"

Joy dried her face and went in to sit on the side of Carole's bed. Briefly, she told her what happened. "Terry is very small for an eight-year-old," Joy said when she had finished her story. "Not a lot taller than Mitzi. And he is thin to the point of being emaciated."

"And Skye didn't say what Terry's problem is?"

"No, only that he hadn't gotten any better. He seemed amazed that Terry had left his room and spoken — even one word. He said the boy hadn't spoken since his mother's death three years ago.

"I want to ask Skye if he will let me see Terry. I seem to fascinate him as much as I frighten him. He must have been the one who was watching me the other evening down in the drawing room."

"You may remind him of his mother," Carole said thoughtfully. "Remember, Jeffrey said she was blonde."

"I remember," Joy said. "Perhaps, in his confused mind, he thinks I am his mother. No . . ." Joy stopped a moment and pondered. "No, I don't really believe he thinks I'm Lillian Windthorn or he wouldn't have been afraid of me. He seemed terrified when I spoke to him and his feet just wouldn't stay put."

Unable to answer their questions, they rang for breakfast. When Washington brought their food and checked on Carole's wrenched knee, Joy asked if she could speak with Skye.

Washington was apologetic. "Mr. Windthorn asked me not to disturb him unless it's an emergency, Mrs. Kyle. He's working on an extremely old leather scroll, and he never likes to be bothered when he's working."

Disappointed, Joy was tempted to see if she could find the boy on her own, but decided against it. They were guests in Skye's home and she really had no right to poke about his house.

Later in the day, she found something that intrigued her. Searching for a needle to sew up a tiny rip in her borrowed robe, she discovered a small photograph face-down in a dresser drawer. A very pretty blonde, blue-eyed young woman smiled at her from the picture. On the back was inscribed: *To Skye, with bunches of love, Lillian.* Joy put it back thoughtfully. Terry did resemble his mother very much.

Washington sent their dinner up at six with a smiling, polite Kim. While eating they listened to the evening newscast on the radio. Both were elated as the radio announcer forecast a let-up in the blizzard by the next day.

"Oh, Joy," Carole confessed, "I love you dearly, but I'm so lonesome for David that I could cry."

"I understand. I'll just be glad to be back with people," Joy said.

"Any certain people?" Carole teased, "such as a good-looking, bearded gentleman whose eyes light up like neon lights when you appear?"

Joy flushed slightly but she laughed. "I do like Jeffrey and I guess it does wonders for my ego that a very eligible bachelor finds me interesting. He quite frankly told me the other day when we were ice-fishing that he plans to see a lot of me."

"You've been holding out on me! How exciting!"

"I'll admit I was flattered," Joy said. "But I'm not sure I want to get emotionally involved just yet. I can make a good living for myself and Mitzi — even though Daddy doesn't want me to work. But I like the feeling of being independent of anyone right now. Is that crazy?"

"Not if that's what you want," Carole declared. "Just tell Jeffrey the truth — that you aren't quite ready to get serious about anyone yet. If he *is* beginning to care for you, he'll wait."

"I-I'm just not sure how I feel about him," Joy said thoughtfully. "He doesn't set my heart to racing, but he does give me a good, secure, cared-for feeling."

"I believe he cares for you," Carole said, "and that is something to be treasured. However, if you don't feel the same way, don't marry him — or anyone — until you do. It's worth waiting for the real thing."

"I keep remembering how madly in love I was with my husband — the rapturous feelings I had. I know he was a heel and a terrible man, but until I really knew what he was, I lived in a golden haze of love. It would be marvelous to love and be loved like that again by someone." She blushed. "Am I a romantic?"

"All of us women are," Carole said.

"You and David have such a happy marriage. I want one like it."

"We do have a good marriage, but we have to work at it. At least I do. David is naturally sweet and loving. He spoils me to death. But you know — before I met Jesus Christ I was so selfish I caused David — and my grandmother — a lot of grief," Carole said frankly. "My willfulness almost cost me David."

"Good, single Christian men aren't found on every street corner," Joy said earnestly, "and Jeffrey seems to be a dedicated Christian man." She laughed. "Maybe I had better latch onto him when we get back." Then she sobered. "If only I knew what I should do. I'm sure he's getting serious about me."

"God knows," Carole said. "I honestly believe if you are sincere and ask Him, He'll show you what to do."

Joy searched Carole's face for a long moment. "You have such a simple faith in God that you inspire me. Would you pray with me right now that God will show me if Jeffrey and I are right for each other?"

After Carole, and then Joy, prayed simple petitions for direction, Joy laughed a trifle shakily. "I'm going to believe I'll have the right answer when the time comes."

"That's trust," Carole said confidently, "and God will honor it, you'll see!"

14

After dinner, Washington brought Carole some crutches he had found in an old storage area. She was delighted and clumped back and forth between their two rooms for exercise. The swelling in her knee was greatly reduced and although it was still very sore, she was grateful to be able to get out of bed.

The two girls decided to go through the lavish wardrobe of the deceased Mrs. Windthorn. Joy found a pair of grey slacks and a pink cotton blouse that fit perfectly, but Carole was not so fortunate. Everything was too large. She finally found a pair of rather worn jeans that she could cinch in with a belt. She topped it with a worn, cotton flannel shirt. Both she found in a sack with other obviously discarded clothing.

Carole was tired by nine that evening, exhausted from the exertion of walking with crutches and trying on clothes. She took a bath, and when Joy came in to say goodnight, she could hear Carole's deep, even breathing and knew she was already asleep. Before she left the room, Joy quietly locked the door and dimmed the lights. She took a leisurely bath, then climbed into bed with a good book she had found in the library yesterday. In no time she was deeply engrossed in her reading.

She read until her eyelids began to droop, then looked at her watch. It was eleven thirty-six. She flipped through the book to see how many pages were left in the chapter. There were several, and suddenly she felt very sleepy.

She laid the book on the nightstand, took off her robe, turned off the light and got back into bed. She felt at peace tonight and intended to spend some time in prayer before she slept, but in just a short while she grew very drowsy. She sank quickly into deep, dreamless sleep.

How long she had been asleep, she didn't know, but something awakened her. She found herself sitting up, every nerve tingling even before she was fully awake.

A high, eerie keen filled the darkness with terrifying sound, erasing even the constant moaning of the storm. The sound was like nothing she had ever heard before. The high-pitched wail rose and fell like the mourning of an animal, echoing through the house like a death knell. She pressed trembling, icy knuckles against her lips and stared wildly into the gloom of the room.

The wail had awakened Carole, too. "Joy, are you all right?" Carole's voice, tinged with panic and fear, reached her through the darkened rooms.

"I'm okay," Joy called. Throwing on her robe, Joy turned on her bedside lamp and hurried into Carole's room.

Carole's dark eyes mirrored Joy's shock and fright. "What is it?"

"I don't know."

"Come get in my bed," Carole said shakily. "I sure don't want to be alone until we find out what's making that s-sound!"

The mourning wail went on and on for several minutes until both girls clapped their hands over their ears trying to shut out the sound.

Suddenly Joy climbed out of bed, slipped her feet in scuffs and went to the door, wrapping her robe about her.

"Where are you going?" Carole asked anxiously.

"It's Terry. I know it is. Something must be horribly wrong. I'm going to see what's going on." Joy's face was pale but determined. And over Carole's protests, she marched out into the hall.

The ululating cry was coming from the same direction as the child had disappeared the night before. Joy's swiftly moving legs were slightly unsteady, her hands clammy cold, and her heart hammering with fright, but the picture in her mind of the small child with fear-filled eyes drew her down the dark corridor. Was someone torturing him?

She turned the corner and quickly passed several doors. A bright light spilled out of a partially open door toward the end of the hallway. The melancholy lament crescendoed as she crept near the end door and she could hear voices — voices she recognized as those of Washington and Skye.

She was almost to the door when Kim came hurrying out and nearly collided with her. Tonight he wasn't smiling. Murmuring an abrupt apology, he hurried away down the hall.

Joy stood in the doorway, her heart still pounding and her throat tight with dread. She clenched her hands together to stop their trembling.

In the bright light Joy saw Washington

bending over a tumbled bed. Skye stood at the foot of it; his face pale and his hair in disarray. Terry was curled into a ball and Joy could see his frail body heaving. The horrifying sounds were pouring in an uninterrupted stream from the child's mouth. Washington was massaging and kneading the child's thin, bare back and shoulders.

Intent upon the boy, neither of the two men noticed Joy in the doorway.

"It looks like we'll have to tranquilize him," Washington spoke with a weary voice. "We've done everything the doctors said might help and, as usual, they don't help a bit."

Joy walked softly across the room. She could see Terry plainly now. His body, though curled into a fetal position around the little ragged, brown stuffed dog, was stiff. His eyes were closed. Her heart quaked as she saw the transparency of the lids over his eyes. His ribs stood out clearly under the pasty-white skin. His mouth was pursed and he seemed to be in a trance-like state as the heartrending sounds poured from him.

Joy felt a lump as big as a boulder in her throat. She took a step closer. "Could I help?"

Two pairs of startled eyes swung in her

direction. Then Skye, his face stern and forbidding, took two steps, grasped her arm and began to steer her from the room. But she pulled her arm away and faced him. Her voice trembled but she steadied it.

"Please let me help. What is wrong with him?"

"You're what's wrong with him!" Skye said savagely. "If you and your nosy friend had stayed at the resort where you belong, this wouldn't have happened!"

"B-but what did we have to do with it?" Joy stammered through stricken lips.

"You remind him of his mother!" Skye spat at her. "He hasn't gone into one of these — these wailing jags in a year or so. In fact, he hasn't even shown any interest in her room for several months — until *you* came here! Now please, Mrs. Kyle, go back to your room and stay out of this! You've done enough harm!" He broke off on almost a sob.

Suddenly the anger and fear that had been building in Joy evaporated. *Skye Windthorn is nearly at the end of his rope,* she thought. Reaching out, she laid a gentle hand on Skye's arm. Her voice was calm and pleading, "Mr. Windthorn, you said I reminded the boy of his mother. I also have a child and I understand your pain.

Please let me try to help."

Skye's eyes were still murderous, so Joy turned to Washington in an appeal for support. "Please let me try."

Washington straightened up, evaluating Joy for a long moment. Nodding slightly to himself he said, "It might be worth a try, Mr. Windthorn. Nothing has helped — the hot bath, the rubdown, nothing. I can't see that it would hurt," he said persuasively.

Suddenly Skye turned away; his shoulders had a defeated slump; his answer was a muttered growl, "See what you can do. But we should probably just give him a shot and get it over with."

Washington moved aside and Joy stepped to the side of the bed. Now that she had permission, she was uncertain what to do. A feeling of helplessness swept over her but she refused to let it linger.

Heavenly Father, tell me what to do. The prayer was silent but as earnest as any she had ever prayed.

Tears prickled in her eyes as she reached out and gathered the stiff, curled child into her arms. He showed no response or resistance. The wail continued to roll from his mouth in echoing waves of hopelessness and despair. Her arms tightened about him and seeing a small wooden rocker in the room, she backed to it and sat down.

She was amazed at how light the un-gainly, stiff bundle in her arms was. Avoiding Washington's sympathetic eyes and the disapproving back that Skye had turned to her, Joy began to sing softly. She sang an old hymn — the first song that came to mind — "Safe in the Arms of Jesus."

For several minutes she sang. There was no sound in the room except her soft crooning and the mournful keening from the child. She was vaguely aware that Kim had reentered the room and was staring at her in astonishment. She shut her eyes to close out the others and prayed silently as she sang.

Dear God, please help this poor child! Still his tortured mind and give him peace and rest. Begin a healing in his spirit and body right now.

The first indication that a change was taking place was a slight relaxation of the boy's body. She could feel him begin to slump against her. Gradually the wails started to subside, first in volume, and then they began to falter, pick up and falter again.

Then abruptly the keening ceased. Joy's heart missed a beat, but she kept her eyes closed and continued to sing softly. She could feel the boy move in her arms and opened her eyes a tiny bit. Terry's blue eyes were open and he was studying her face intently. She closed her eyes again, sensing that it would never do for Terry to see her watching him.

Even though she continued to sing, a part of her was tense. What would Terry do now? Would he jump from her arms and run? She felt him move and her heart quivered. Then she felt his soft touch on her face and she heard his softly breathed, "mamma." It was so soft she was sure no one else had heard it.

For a long moment, she felt the boy's gaze on her face. Then with a faint little sigh, Terry sank back against her. Though her arms ached from supporting his weight, she held him until she felt him completely relax against her and heard his regular, even breathing.

Tentatively she opened her eyes. The frail child was sound asleep, the tattered stuffed dog still clutched to his small, skinny chest.

When she made a move to rise, Skye and Washington were instantly beside her. Supporting her on both sides, they helped her up, and without them, she would surely have fallen. Her legs and arms were so cramped from sitting in one position for untold minutes that she could hardly stand.

She crossed the room on slightly wobbly legs, and let Skye gently lay the boy on his bed. Apparently exhausted, Terry hugged the tattered brown dog to his body and sighed sleepily as Joy drew the covers up around his bony little shoulders. Joy held her breath as his eyelids fluttered faintly. Then Terry snuggled down into the blanket and continued to breathe steadily and deeply.

The four adults tiptoed to the door. Washington switched off the light, leaving only a faint nightlight on and the door slightly ajar.

They retreated down the hall past a couple of doors before anyone spoke.

"Can you beat that!" Washington exclaimed softly.

Joy felt slightly heady with success and relief. "Thank God!" she said reverently.

"Thank you!" Skye's eyes were alight with excitement as he faced Joy, his expression transformed by relief. "That's the first time anything has brought him out of one of these crying sessions except a strong tranquilizer."

Joy laughed. "Mothers have been rocking babies for thousands of years. It's a very old remedy."

Skye's eyes were a warm, smoky grey when he wasn't angry, Joy noticed. They remained thoughtfully upon her now. "Mrs. Kyle, I owe you an apology for my abominable behavior. I'm sorry."

"Forget it." Joy said. "You were worried about your son."

Those smoky grey eyes remained locked with hers. "I appreciate your understanding, but I feel I owe you an explanation about Terry's sickness, if you would care to hear it."

"If you're sure, I would like that."

"It's chilly out here in the hall. Let's go down to the library. I was working there until just a short while ago so it should still be warm. Washington, would you sleep in the room adjoining Terry's tonight, in case he needs you? Kim, please bring us some coffee before you retire."

"I'll need to let Carole know that everything is all right. She's awake and will be worrying," Joy said.

"Fine, I'll go on down and stir up the fire in the fireplace."

When Joy entered Carole's room, she was sitting in a chair, a bathrobe drawn over her pajamas and the crutches propped in easy reach. Her lovely face was drawn and pale. "Joy!" she exclaimed. "I was giving you five more minutes and then I was coming after you! I've been worried to death. What happened?"

Joy filled her in on the story briefly and concluded, "I'm meeting Skye down in the library where there's a fire — the hall is like a freezer. He said he would explain about Terry's condition."

Carole sounded thoughtful as she replied, "Mr. Windthorn seems to be thawing toward you."

"He really can be quite nice when he wants to be."

"He can also be quite an ogre," Carole said dryly. "Please don't stay late. That man scares me. How do you know *he* isn't responsible for Terry's nightmares?"

Joy laughed gaily. "I do declare, you're as bad as a doting mother! But I promise to not be late." She went out the door with a carefree wave.

15

A fresh log blazed in the fireplace, casting a warm glow into the spacious room, when Joy entered the library. She loved books and seeing the walls lined with volumes of every description filled her with delight The cheery fire added to the charm of the room. Skye had drawn two comfortable looking leather chairs close to the fireplace and placed a small table between.

The cookies and steaming pot of coffee Kim was laying out on the small table looked and smelled delicious. Kim set out small plates, heavy mugs, silverware and paper napkins. Then with a flash of white teeth in Joy's direction and a polite "good-night," he withdrew.

Prince lay on a small rug near the fireplace. He lifted his head when Joy entered the room and watched her until she was seated, then languidly lowered his head and closed his eyes. Joy suppressed a shudder, recalling her harrowing encounter with the huge beast.

Skye waved Joy to a chair and seated himself in the other. "Washington does the cooking but cookies are Kim's specialty," he said with a slight smile. "And, we're in luck; he just made a batch this evening. Snickerdoodles, oatmeal crispies — and that delicate-looking one is my favorite, angel food cookies made with coconut. Help yourself. How do you take your coffee?"

"Just a dash of cream. I didn't know I was hungry until I saw those cookies and smelled the coffee," Joy said. She accepted the cup of coffee Skye handed her and selected one each of the cookies.

She was aware that Skye was studying her as she sipped her coffee and munched cookies but for some reason she was not uncomfortable. She raised her eyes and met his across the small table. Again she noticed how warm his grey eyes were when he wasn't angry. *Skye is really a very attractive man*, she thought in surprise, an unfamiliar feeling stirring in her.

"The storm should end in a day or so now," Skye said, breaking into her thoughts. "That means you can get back to your resort soon." He paused and sipped his coffee. Setting the cup down, he leaned toward her and said abruptly, "But I've a proposal to make you. Would you consider staying on a few days and working with Terry?"

Joy recalled her intense desire a day or so before to try to help the child and she was glad now that she hadn't been able to talk to Skye about it. He probably would have refused before tonight. She hesitated, and Skye continued.

"I would be glad to pay you anything you ask." He smiled apologetically. "Frankly, I haven't wanted a woman around, but perhaps a woman's touch is what Terry needs. I know it's asking a lot but. . . ."

"Perhaps, you could tell me something about Terry and his problems before I decide," Joy said cautiously.

"That's fair," Skye said, although he hesitated just a moment. Unnamed emotions flitted across his face as he spoke. "As I told you before, Terry hasn't spoken since his mother's death. He has a very poor appetite, and is afraid of nearly everything. He's even been afraid of leaving his room and is simply petrified at the thought of leaving the house."

"That's why you didn't think anyone could have been watching us behind the drawing room curtain the other night and why Washington thought I was dreaming about a child entering my room?"

"Right. Terry must have been fascinated when he heard the voice of a woman in the house. His curiosity apparently overcame his fear."

"Terry doesn't leave his room at all, then?"

"Very seldom. Last week, however, he has slipped into my study twice and removed a small marble statue that I use as a paperweight. It was given to me in Greece by an old man I befriended. Each time it disappeared, Washington found it the next day in Terry's room."

"Why do you think Terry took the statue?" Joy asked. "Does it mean something special to him?"

"I don't know for sure. He has never taken anything from my office before. But perhaps the carved marble goddess head reminded Terry of his mother. He idolized her."

"Did he seem disturbed when Washington took it away?"

"No. According to Washington, the boy seemed surprised when Washington found it — hidden in his bed — the first time. Terry examined it like he had never seen it before. I almost wonder if he was walking in his sleep both times when he took it. Or it could be an act. I'm never sure if part of Terry's illness is a play to get sympathy."

"The doctors haven't been able to help Terry?"

Skye's grey eyes darkened as with pain, and he shifted them to the blazing log. "I have had Terry in two hospitals, the local one and then in a large children's hospital in Seattle. Both times he grew rapidly worse, crying and moaning as he did tonight, almost continually, and wouldn't eat at all.

"The only thing that calmed him was a promise to take him home so the doctor suggested that I try it. So I flew him home and he's been here ever since. But I've had a series of specialists flown here over the past three years with no lasting results. At times he's a little better — he's even learned to read, write and do arithmetic under Washington's tutorage. He's an avid reader during his good times, and he reads way beyond his age level."

"And Terry was completely normal before the accident?"

"Absolutely." Bitterness crept into his voice. "Lillian was a poor excuse for a wife, but she did love Terry. She spoiled him and was inclined to make a baby of him, but for the chance he had, he was a normal child: bright, happy and mischievous."

"Were you able to be with Terry much before his mother's death?"

Skye sighed. "Not much. I blame myself now for that. I guess I felt that a five-year-old mainly needed a mother. I was away a lot with my work, and when I was home, I was very busy." He paused. "I didn't know the boy very well, although he did seem pleased when I was home."

Pain shadowed his face. "But from the day Lillian died, Terry has seemed to dislike me — maybe is even afraid of me. He seems to shrink into a shell when I'm around. He decidedly prefers Washington — and even Kim — to me. I have wondered if Lillian deliberately turned him against me at the last." He hesitated as if the next words were difficult to say, "Or perhaps he feels that I'm in some way responsible for his mother's death."

"Your wife didn't like to travel with you in your work?"

Anger and bitterness burned in Skye's expressive eyes, and his voice became harsh.

"Lillian refused to ever accompany me! The conditions I work under are not always the best, but some accommodations

140

were such that she and Terry would have been quite comfortable. Believe me, I wanted them with me!"

His short laugh was derisive. "Lillian liked to travel, all right, but only to parties where there were lots of men to admire her. She was a cheap little flirt," he ended savagely.

"Were you here when the accident occurred?" Joy asked softly, moved by Skye's unexpected openness and vulnerability.

"Yes and no. I had returned home just that evening and found the house full of people — a weekend party. My best friend, Bob Scholes, was one of the guests." Skye's eyes were bleak as he continued.

"I was furious that Lillian had planned a party when she knew I was coming home and would be tired. I had been away for three months and wanted to be alone with my wife and son. We quarreled — about the party."

"Did Terry hear you quarreling?"

"Not that I know of, but I'm afraid half the county could have heard me. We had a horrible fight. I accused her of being a flirt and a lot of other things." Skye's voice tightened. "I said some pretty nasty things, I'm afraid. I have an abominable temper and in the thick of the quarrel, I demanded

141

to know if she had been unfaithful to me. She told me I was driving her to it. Then I said something dreadful. I was angry and wanted to hurt her and . . . it just popped out."

Skye's face was pale and Joy saw a muscle twitch in his jaw.

"You don't need to tell me these things, if it bothers you," she said gently.

"If you're to help Terry, I want you to get a picture of how it all happened, and I've had to live with the agony of my words for three long years."

Skye took a deep breath and then continued, "I told her, 'How do I even know if Terry is mine, you little flirt! Maybe one of your admirers is his father!' "

Joy gasped. "But surely you don't believe that?"

"I don't know what I believe," Skye said defeatedly. "But it really doesn't matter now. Whether he's mine or not, the boy is my responsibility."

He paused and looked directly at Joy. "Maybe I hit the nail on the head, because Lillian burst into tears and ran from the room. Later that night she and Bob left in my light plane, and it crashed before it got completely off the ground."

"Maybe she wasn't running away with

your friend," Joy suggested. "Perhaps your wife just asked him to take her away from Windthorn."

"I would like to have believed that, but she made a public announcement to her guests that she was leaving me for Bob. That she and Bob had been in love for a long time and she should have left me long ago. Washington said she — and Bob — had been drinking pretty heavily that night. He shouldn't have tried to fly a plane."

"You heard the announcement — that she was leaving you for Bob?"

"No. When Lillian ran from the room, I left the house in a rage. I drove to town and checked into a hotel room. I was there a few hours later when Washington called from the hospital and told me of the plane crash — and that Lillian and Bob were dead.

"Washington flies, and he had used my helicopter to bring Terry into the hospital. I raced over there but the boy was in a state of shock. He was dazed and couldn't speak. The only emotion he seemed capable of was — fear. He seemed afraid of me and wouldn't even let me touch him. When I tried to talk to him, he went into an awful moaning spell like you saw tonight.

"The doctor gave him a shot that put him to sleep. He thought the child would be all right, given a little time and a lot of care. But he wasn't."

"Who found the child?"

"Lillian's guests had all retired for the night. Washington heard the crash and rushed out. He found Terry wandering near the crashed plane. He was confused and frightened — and he couldn't say a word."

"Terry was in the plane, too, then, and thrown clear?"

"Everyone presumed so. And Terry couldn't talk and tell anyone. Later, he went into hysterics if anyone tried to talk to him about the crash.

"After a week at our local hospital, Terry still couldn't talk and seemed to be getting worse by the day. So I flew him in my helicopter to a hospital in Seattle and got the best doctors money could provide — specialists — to treat him. But he had one of those crying fits nearly every day, wouldn't eat and just grew worse.

"That's when one doctor suggested he might do better at home — and I concurred. So I brought him home. We've had some bad times with him, but overall, he does do better here. Sometimes he seems to be quite content. At other times he lapses into listlessness, won't eat, and seems to be brooding."

"Do you think his main problem might be that he still misses his mother terribly?"

"Possibly. When nothing else seems to bring him out of his listless state, Washington takes him to his mother's room."

"That's why the room has been left as it was when she died?"

"Yes. Terry curls up on her bed with that ridiculous brown stuffed dog and stays for a few hours. After a while he's ready to go back to his room. However, for several months, he hasn't wanted to go to his mother's room and this is the first wailing spell he has suffered in better than a year."

"I can see why you were so upset when Carole and I landed on your doorstep. I am truly sorry if we've caused your son to have a relapse."

Skye chuckled suddenly to Joy's astonishment. "Just when I was sure I had run you off for good!" But the teasing light faded quickly from his eyes. "Seriously, though, even if Terry hasn't had any crying fits or felt a need for the solace of his mother's room, he still is not much better."

Skye's face was very grave, "I don't know where else to go or what else to do. I've spent so much money on doctors that I had to sell part of my property as well as dispose of some other assets. And still Terry is very little, if any, better."

His eyes were filled with pain. "Terry is like a living dead person. There are days when I feel it would have been better for the child if he had died in that crash, too."

Joy was shocked but held her peace.

Skye closed his eyes and wearily sank his head into his hands. After a moment he raised his head and looked at Joy. "*Could* there be something Terry is brooding about? Something, perhaps, that he knows or saw that is tearing him apart? Something we don't know about?

"That's what I was hoping you could find out. You are the only one he has spoken to in three years. If only you could get him to talk — to release his feelings — his fears — perhaps talk about the plane crash and his mother's death. Maybe then we would have something to work on. Would you be willing to try?"

"It's scary to try something like this," Joy said honestly, "when even the specialists have failed. But I would like to try. Just don't get your hopes up too much. I might not be able to accomplish anything. He was terrified of me the other night when I spoke to him and he ran out of the room like I was the living embodiment of his worst nightmare."

"All I ask is that you try," Skye said.

"When shall I start?"

"In the morning as soon as you get up, if that's not too soon. We could have breakfast brought to his room for you both."

"Breakfast it is," Joy said as she rose to go. "And give my compliments to Kim on his excellent cookies."

When Joy arrived back at her room, she switched on the light and stood still for a moment, savoring the beauty of the fairy princess room. Suddenly her heart missed a beat. The large waterfall picture was gone! She went over to the wall. A faint outline remained to show where it had hung.

Joy's eyes swept the room but the picture had vanished. A quiver of alarm ran through her. Someone had been in here while she was away! Carole! Was Carole all right?

Joy hurried through the connecting hall and tapped on Carole's door. Relief surged through her when Carole answered.

Joy pushed open the door and Carole, sitting up in bed with a book on her lap, exclaimed, "Come in and tell about your chat with Skye! I'm dying of curiosity!"

"Did you hear anyone in my room, while I was out?" Joy asked.

"No, why?"

"That large picture of a waterfall is gone." She shrugged. "Maybe Kim or Washington took it for some reason. It really doesn't matter. Let me tell you the news!"

Briefly, Joy summarized Skye's revelations about Terry and of her decision to try to help him.

"That sounds like a big order," Carole said. "If trained specialists have not been able to help the child. . . ." She left it hanging for a moment. Then said, "I'm sorry, Joy, that wasn't faith talking. You 'can do all things through Christ who strengthens us.' God has promised us wisdom if we ask, so let's pray that God will direct you and be with you in dealing with Terry."

16

Joy looked over toward Terry's bed for perhaps the fiftieth time since she had arrived an hour ago. She was trying to read but couldn't keep her mind on the book in her lap. Terry was still sound asleep, looking pale and fragile as he lay there. Clad in blue pajamas, his skinny little frame scarcely lifted the blankets from the bed. His breathing barely moved the colorful blanket. His limp blond hair was tumbled, and he clutched his tattered brown dog to his thin chest even in sleep.

Even though Joy had awakened early this morning and spent a long time in prayer and the Word of God, Joy had come into Terry's room almost trembling and with questions tumbling about in her mind. How would Terry react when he saw Joy in his room? Would he go into one of those dreadful moaning spells? What should she say to the boy?

Suddenly a Scripture popped into her mind. "Be not afraid nor dismayed . . . the battle is not yours, but God's."

Excitement flowed through her. She repeated the verse in her mind, savoring its meaning. *That's right,* she thought. *Carole and I both have prayed, and given the problem of Terald Windthorn to God! So what is there to worry about?*

Resolutely opening the book she had brought with her, she began to read again. But the strange little boy, a few yards away from her, was so much more real than the characters in the story that it was hard to keep her mind on the words.

Restlessly Joy laid the book aside and went to stand at the window. Rubbing the moisture from the glass, she looked out into a North Pole wonderland. A deep layer of glistening white covered everything. Heavy, snow laden boughs of spruce, pine and fir were drooping under their loads. The snow was still coming down but the weatherman was predicting that the worst of the storm was over.

Joy smiled slightly as she recalled with pleasure the friendly, companionable chat she had shared with Skye last night. And Carole said that Skye had sent Kim with cookies and coffee for her, also, last night.

How thoughtful! And he seemed to love Terry deeply — even though he wasn't sure Terry was his son. Admirable qualities. Skye was far from all bad.

She remembered the warmth in those smoky grey eyes when Skye had talked with her last night and felt a glow start in the vicinity of her heart and spread deliciously over her whole body.

Suddenly Joy brought her thoughts up short. *This will never do,* she told herself sternly. *Just because Skye was civil to you means only one thing: He thinks you might be able to help his son. Nothing more. And don't you forget it!*

A slight sound broke Joy's reverie. She dropped the heavy curtain and turned.

Terry was awake — and staring at her with wide, startled eyes filled with terror.

For a full moment Joy stared back at him, her heart beating with dismay at the stark fear in his eyes. A frantic question beat in her brain. *What has happened to this child to create such desperate fear in his heart?* Was he an abused child? Had Skye vented his venom — for his unfaithful wife — on her helpless son? Surely not! The thought was ghastly and terrifying. If he had, he wouldn't be seeking help for him, would he?

But the "whys" and "hows" weren't the problem right now. Joy took hold of her emotions. She stood very still. Pitching her voice low, she said softly, "Terry, don't be afraid. I'm not going to hurt you. I've just come to visit you."

Terry flicked his eyes toward the door and then back to her.

He looks just like a cornered little animal who's about to be pounced on by a mountain lion, Joy thought in horror.

"Terry . . ." Her mind groped for the right words — the words that would halt the mad dash for refuge that she could see in Terry's furtive, frightened glances toward the doorway. "Terry — Jesus doesn't want you to be afraid."

A barely perceptible change flitted across Terry's face at the word "Jesus."

Joy's heart quickened. Somewhere in Terry's short life someone had told him about Jesus! She grasped the straw. "Jesus loves you, Terry — and He loves me."

Was the fear fading from the child's eyes? Although still poised for flight, he seemed to be listening to her words.

"My name is Joy," she continued softly. "I have a little girl who isn't much smaller than you." Joy smiled. "She has a big cat named Ebenezer. What's your dog's name?"

Terry just stared at Joy with wide blue eyes.

"I had a stuffed dog when I was a little girl," Joy continued. "Only he was pure white. I called him Snowball. I guess a good name for your dog would be Brownie. Is that what you call him?"

Terry's eyes moved slowly down to rest on the lop-eared, bedraggled stuffed dog in his arms. The words were a whisper but to Joy's ears they could have been a shout. "Sparky is his name."

Joy strove to keep the elation that surged up in her from showing in her voice. "Sparky, I like that name."

The fear was gone from Terry's eyes now, but they were still wary and his body was stiffly alert.

Joy cast her eyes about the room, looking for something to talk about that might interest the boy. One side of the room was lined with shelves of books, hundreds of them. "I see you like to read, Terry. So do I."

Tentatively, she moved slowly across the room, watching him from the corner of her eye as she went and continuing to talk in an unemotional but friendly tone. "You surely do have a lot of books. I wonder if you have anything that I've read."

Terry was out of her line of vision now. Joy's heart began to do flip-flops. Would Terry bolt and run, now that her eyes weren't on him? She forced the thought from her mind and continued to talk softly as she ran exploring fingers over the edges of the books. "You've got *Robin Hood* — and *Tom Sawyer*. They're two of my favorites."

Joy pulled out *Robin Hood* and turned toward Terry. He was watching her every move with a curious, fascinated expression on his face.

"When I was little I used to wish I was a boy," Joy confided. "I lived in a huge old house, a lot like yours, and. . . ."

"You . . . look . . . like . . . my . . . mother." The words were spoken slowly, and almost as if Terry were speaking to himself.

"Yes, I know." Joy tried to speak calmly over the tumult of excitement bubbling up inside her. She laid the book on a table. "Her hair was blonde and she had blue eyes like mine." She glanced down at the pink blouse and grey tailored slacks she was wearing. "These clothes are your mother's. I hope you don't mind. I don't have any extra clothes with me."

Terry said nothing but continued to stare at her as if mesmerized. The only at-

154

tractive feature on his wizened face were his clear, beautiful blue eyes.

"Did you know that you look like your mother, Terry?"

"Did you know my mother?"

"No, I saw a picture of her — in her room."

"She was pretty — like you." Terry spoke matter of factly.

"Your father said your mother loved you very much."

At the mention of Skye, Terry's face changed abruptly and Joy was astonished to see the bitterness and anger that twisted the small boy's features. Amazingly, he strongly resembled his father when his face registered those emotions.

"He made my mother c-cry — and I hate him!"

Joy was shocked at the vehemence behind the words. "That was a long time ago, Terry," Joy said gently. "And your father loves you very much."

"No, he doesn't!" He dropped his eyes as if ashamed of the malice that smoldered there but faintly defiant, too.

Joy didn't like the turn the conversation was taking. Terry was trembling and his face was drained of any color. She must get him on another subject.

"Let's forget about all that and have some breakfast. What do you say? I'm starved."

Terry lifted indifferent, moody eyes to hers.

"I'm not hungry, but Washington will bring you something, if you want it." A sulkiness had crept into his expression.

Joy wondered uneasily if Terry didn't eat sometimes as a weapon to worry and punish his father. What grudge did he hold against Skye? Surely more than the spoken one. However, making his mother cry might be reason enough in a child's mind, if allowed to fester.

"Would you ring Washington for me, then?" Joy said, as cheerfully as she could.

Without answering, Terry reached for the buzzer beside his bed.

Washington must have been hovering nearby because he was tapping on the door within a minute.

Joy noticed that as he entered, Washington's keen dark eyes went swiftly to her face and then Terry's.

"Ready for breakfast?" he asked, smiling.

Terry shook his head indifferently, but Joy said with more animation than she felt, "Yes, I'm ready — and why don't you bring a little something for Terry, too. In case he's hungry when he sees mine."

The meal Washington brought was a feast. There were crusty, homemade hot biscuits, brown sausage patties, fluffy scrambled eggs, orange juice, sliced red tomatoes, blackberry jelly, and a small pot of hot chocolate, besides steaming coffee.

Washington brought a small folding table from a closet and set it up. Over it he spread a bright yellow tablecloth. He took dishes and silverware from a cupboard.

"We can take it from here," Joy said. "And the meal looks delicious."

Washington started to protest, seemed to think better of it and withdrew, after telling them to ring when they wanted the dishes removed.

"Run and wash your hands and face," she said as soon as Washington had gone. "There is way too much food here for one person to eat."

Terry shook his head and muttered something that sounded like, "Don't want anything to eat."

"Suit yourself," Joy said, trying to sound indifferent. She went into his bathroom and washed her face and hands.

Drawing a chair up to the table, she started to sit down. She glanced up and saw Terry's eyes watching her every move.

Turning around she put one hand on her hip and drew her mouth and brows down in an exaggerated frown, "How can I eat with you and Sparky gawking at me? Either come and eat or turn around so I can't see your eyes!"

Terry looked somewhat shocked. When she continued to glare at him, and hold to that ridiculous stance, he suddenly giggled.

Joy grinned. "Go on and laugh but I'm bigger than you so I can make you mind me!"

Terry giggled again and then laughed outright. The laugh sounded a bit strange, like he wasn't accustomed to exercising those particular muscles.

He slid slowly off the bed, still gripping his stuffed dog and made for the bathroom. Joy heard water splashing and in a couple of minutes he was back. He had even combed his unruly hair.

Terry dragged a chair up to the table and climbed onto it.

"Since I'm your guest, you're supposed to serve my plate," Joy said, her eyes twinkling. She picked up a plate and passed it to him.

He took it solemnly and looked questioningly at her.

"I'll have some of everything," she said.

Gravely and not as awkwardly as she would have expected, Terry filled her plate and passed it back to her.

"Thank you," Joy said. "I love hot biscuits, don't you?" She split one, put a pat of butter between the halves and took a bite. "Hmmmm, it's as good as I thought it would be!"

Terry watched her for a moment as she began to eat. Then, he reached for a plate. He didn't eat a large meal, but he did eat a little of everything while Joy carried on a mainly one-sided conversation about books and games and anything else that came to her mind.

Much of the time he simply watched her face, as if he couldn't get enough of her. It could have been unnerving, but Joy knew the lonely boy was only seeing his idolized mother in her.

As they were finishing breakfast, Joy said, "Who told you about Jesus, Terry?"

Terry put his head on one side, obviously considering. "I had a nurse once — a long, long time ago. Her skin was black like Washington's and her hair was white. I called her Aunt Sally and she called me Baby. She read me stories about Jesus." He paused and looked sad. "Mamma said she was too old to do a good job, so she didn't

159

get to stay very long. But she left me her story book and I read out of it sometimes."

Thank you, Lord, Joy thought, *for that nameless lady who planted some seeds in this young heart. With your help, I will try to water and cultivate them and perhaps there will be a harvest yet.*

17

When Washington came for Terry's classes a short while later, they almost had a rebellion on their hands. Although Terry didn't say a word in Washington's presence, he had had long practice in communicating his wishes and dislikes without words. As soon as Washington appeared and Joy excused herself to go, Terry went into a sulk and rudely turned his back on Joy and Washington.

Joy felt like spanking him. But instead, she walked over and spoke gently, "Terry, you remember at breakfast that I said my friend, Carole, has hurt her knee badly. Well, I must go now and see about her and visit with her a while or she'll be lonely. When your lessons are over, I'll come back. Washington will let me know. Okay?"

Terry stubbornly refused to look at Joy, his face pouty and angry.

"Very well, young man," Joy allowed a little of the exasperation she was feeling to creep into her voice, "if you don't want me to come back, I won't!"

She turned away and moved toward the door. "Washington, I'll see you later."

Before she reached the door, Terry jumped up, ran to her, and caught her hand.

Joy turned back and said carefully, "Oh, you want me to come back?"

Terry continued to cling to her hand, his face the picture of wretchedness.

Joy slowly shook her head, "I can't stay, but I promise to come back for lunch — and we'll play a game, if you like. But you must have your lessons now," she said firmly. "And you'll be a good student this morning, won't you?" On an impulse, Joy stooped and touched his cheek lightly with her lips.

Terry reluctantly released her hand, but followed her to the door. He didn't step out into the hall but when Joy reached the corner and looked back, his head was still visible, watching her around the door casing. She lifted her hand and saw his hand come out and give a dispirited wave.

When Joy rounded the corner and started toward her room, she saw Skye standing at the head of the stairs, obviously waiting for her. When she drew near, he moved down the hall to meet her.

Skye's expression was withdrawn and remote today, and his eyes were slightly bloodshot as if he hadn't slept much. He stopped a couple of feet from her. His voice sounded strained, "How did it go?"

"Not bad," Joy said. "When Terry first woke up and saw me there, I think it upset him. But I talked quietly to him, and he gradually settled down."

"Did he talk to you?"

"He didn't talk a great deal but he did talk."

"Did you learn anything?"

"Not really," Joy said cautiously. "I tried to go slowly so he wouldn't clam up on me. The only reason he talks to me, I'm sure, is because I remind him so much of his mother."

"It's strange that the boy talks to you when he hasn't talked to anyone else for three years." Skye frowned. "Do you think he's just been pretending he can't talk?"

"I don't know, at this point." She hesitated and then said candidly, "Mr. Windthorn, if Terry knew you had asked me to — to work with him, I don't think he would have anything more to do with me." As soon as the words were out, she knew her wording had not been good because Skye took the words as a personal affront.

"Then it's true that Terry detests me for some reason — isn't it?" His voice had grown harsh and his face formidable.

Joy took a long breath. When Skye Windthorn looked so fierce and spoke so caustically, he was frightening. "Yes," her voice came out a little squeaky and she cleared her throat and tried again, "Yes, he does seem to dislike you. The only reason he gave, though, was that you made his mother cry."

Skye's jaw tightened and Joy could sense the fury that smoldered behind those bleak eyes fixed upon her.

"It wasn't enough that she was unfaithful to me," he grated out, "but she had to turn the boy against me, too."

"Perhaps she didn't turn Terry against you," Joy said.

Skye's head snapped up and his eyes glittered with anger, "If she didn't, who did?" he said scornfully.

Joy swallowed hard. Skye reminded her so much of her own tyrannical father when she was a child. She and her mother had lived in constant fear of arousing his anger. And in the few months of her marriage to Ferron Kyle — before he had left her — Joy had lived in fear of his displeasure, too. She was experiencing the same, agonizing feelings, now.

Then, suddenly, her head went up and she looked straight into those derisive, stony eyes. "Mr. Windthorn, maybe you frighten Terry to death. If I were a child, I would certainly be frightened of you now."

One of Skye's eyebrows shot up and suddenly the wrath vanished from his eyes and face. Twin twinkles danced there. He chuckled and then laughed aloud. "As I told you last night, I have an abominable temper. I apologize. I had no reason to take my hostility out on you." His eyes on her had grown warm and filled with dancing lights. "And I like a girl with spirit! Will you accept my apology?"

"Of course, forget it," Joy heard herself saying. His eyes upon her were as warm as a caress and she found it impossible to remain angry.

Joy felt her color begin to rise as Skye continued to study her face in that curiously intent way he had, as if he were scrutinizing an intensely interesting artifact.

Abruptly he spoke. "Do you think Mrs. Loring would feel like coming down to join you and me at dinner tonight? Washington tells me she is getting about quite well on the crutches."

Surprised, Joy answered, "I'm sure she would. And that is very kind of you."

"Good! I'll have Washington prepare something special since I will be entertaining two such lovely ladies."

Joy was not sure if Skye was mocking himself or them but she decided not to worry about it. Surely she and Carole would be more than a match for one man, even one whose moods seemed as mercurial as Skye Windthorn's.

18

Carole was pleased at the prospect of going downstairs for dinner. "It will be rather interesting to see Skye Windthorn when he isn't angry or insolent," she remarked.

"He can be quite charming when he wants to be," Joy assured her. "And yet he can be bitter and sarcastic in almost the next breath. He's a complex, perplexing man."

"I do appreciate his taking us in like this, though," mused Carole. "I'm sure it's at his request that Washington and Kim have given us such marvelous treatment."

"And he does love his son very much. It distresses him no end that Terry seems to dislike him."

"He appears to be confiding in you quite freely." There was a teasing light in Carole's dark eyes. "The charms of the master of Windthorn aren't causing you to forget a very nice bearded gentleman who is waiting for you back at Forest Lakes Lodge, is he?"

To her dismay, Joy felt a wave of heat wash into her face, and she answered a little too hastily — and much too vehemently, "Skye Windthorn could never in a thousand years come close to being the sweet, kind man that Jeffrey is! I've had my fill of Skye Windthorn's kind for one lifetime!"

Carole's expressive eyebrows rose. "I was just teasing, Joy. But, seriously, I would be greatly alarmed if I thought you might be falling for Skye. You aren't, are you?"

Joy turned away and went to stand at the window, pushing aside the heavy drapes to stare out at the ice and snow and jagged icicles. Idly, she noticed that the blizzard was in full cry again. And the weatherman had said the storm was about over!

Joy let the velvety drape fall back into place and turned back to Carole. When Joy spoke, her voice held bewilderment. "I know it's crazy — and unwise — and illogical, b-but I am attracted to Skye. It frightens me." She bit her lip in consternation. "Do you suppose there are some people who always fall for someone who isn't good for them?"

"It does seem so," Carole admitted. "But

I think we can keep our heads and refuse to let the feeling grow, if we see it's unwise, don't you?"

"Yes, I do!" Joy smiled suddenly, "However, I haven't fallen in love with Skye — yet. And I don't plan to let that happen," she ended decisively. "Not only because of his moods, but," she said, her voice growing softer, "I know Skye isn't a Christian and I don't want to marry anyone who doesn't love the Lord. I have to be able to share the most important part — and Person — of my life."

"Good! You had me worried there for a moment! God always honors our faithfulness, Joy. You'll be glad you waited for His best."

At noon, Kim came with a tray for Carole and a message that Joy's lunch would be served in Terry's room.

"I feel guilty running off and leaving you alone all the time," Joy told Carole.

"You run along and don't fret about me," Carole reassured her. "If you can help that little boy, it will be worth a great deal of sacrifice on all our parts. Besides," she grinned, "I have a super mystery book started, and I'm dying to find out who the villain is."

"I'm glad to know I can be replaced so

easily," Joy said in mock indignation.

Carole aimed a pillow at Joy's retreating back.

When Joy entered Terry's large, cozy room a few minutes later, she could tell that he was a bit miffed at her. But she ignored his slightly aggrieved air and went immediately to the wall that was lined from ceiling to floor with books.

"Which ones are your favorites?" she said over her shoulder to Terry.

For a moment it seemed that he was going to ignore her question, then she heard his step behind her and he moved to stand by her side. Glancing down, she noted with pleasure that he looked better — much better. Looking more closely, she saw that he was dressed in brown corduroy trousers, a yellow knit shirt and brown and yellow athletic shoes. His neatly combed hair had a faint sheen to it as if it had been freshly shampooed and a bit of hair dressing applied.

Terry dressed up for me! she thought suddenly. A lump as big as a snowball formed in her throat.

She turned to face him. "My, don't you look sharp!"

His thin lips curved into a pleased, crooked grin and a slight flush rose into his pale face. "Thanks," he said. The sullen look was gone and his blue eyes, still looking too large for his pinched face, glowed.

Terry pulled a book from a shelf. "I like this one but it's got some hard words, so I haven't read too much of it yet." It was clearly an invitation for Joy to read to him.

"Would you like me to read some of it to you after lunch?" Joy asked innocently.

"Would you?"

"Right after lunch. By the way, what are we having for lunch?"

"Toasted cheese sandwiches and cream of asparagus soup," Terry replied. His face clouded suddenly and he said anxiously, "Is that all right? If you don't like that I'll get Washing . . ."

"That's just fine," Joy interrupted. "In fact, it sounds super. I'm hungry, aren't you?"

Before Terry could answer, Kim arrived with their lunch. Apparently Terry was accustomed to being waited on and he made no move to help as Kim set up the table and brought dishes from the cupboard.

"I think Terry and I would like to set the table," Joy suddenly said.

Kim looked uncertainly from one to the other. "I really don't mind doing it, miss."

Terry motioned for Kim to leave the room and, looking slightly puzzled, Kim complied.

Terry now took over and began to move briskly around the little table, laying out dishes and silverware. He even brought a graceful, white porcelain swan and placed it in the center for a centerpiece.

"Who showed you how to set a proper table, Terry?" Joy asked in astonishment.

"I've watched Kim and Washington all my life," he said airily. "I should know how it's done."

"You're also a cocky little twerp," Joy said, cushioning the comment with a grin.

Terry was too pleased with himself to be abashed.

When the meal was over and Kim had taken away the dishes, Joy settled herself in the comfortable rocking chair and opened the book Terry brought to her. Terry settled himself nearby on the luxurious orange and gold shag rug with a large floor pillow at his back.

Suddenly Joy was aware that, for the first time, Terry had not picked up his ragged stuffed dog since she had entered the room. It lay on the pillows of his bed. Was it significant that he seemed to feel no need of it this afternoon? She hoped so.

The book was the Rudyard Kipling classic, *Captains Courageous*. Joy found, as the story unfolded, that she was enjoying it as much as Terry seemed to be. Once in a while he would interrupt her for the explanation of a word, and Joy was astonished at the intelligence that the eight-year-old unwittingly displayed through his questions and quick grasp of her explanations.

This child was far from the "living dead" that his father had described him to be.

After reading steadily for an hour, Joy suggested they take a break and have some of the chilled apple juice she had seen in the tiny refrigerator tucked away next to the dish cupboard. To her delight, Terry also produced a bag of ruffled potato chips.

Joy sat on the floor facing Terry and drew a large pillow to her back. They sipped the tangy juice and crunched potato chips companionably for a few minutes while Terry explained how to play a game he had produced from a closet stuffed with games of every description.

They spread the game out on a low table between them and began to play, both sitting crossed-legged on the floor.

Terry's eyes sparkled triumphantly when he won the first game.

"You won't beat me so easily this time,"

Joy vowed, as they prepared to play again. "I have the hang of it, now."

But Terry won again, though not as readily.

When Joy exclaimed, "I'll beat you yet," and began to stir the pieces with unwonted violence, Terry bounded up and down and crowed with glee.

Then suddenly he sobered and looked at her anxiously, "You really don't mind — that you lost — do you?"

Joy grimaced and said with mock anger, "Of course, I mind, you rapscallion, you!"

Terry shouted — actually shouted — with laughter. When he could get his breath again, he asked, "What's a rapscallion?"

Joy couldn't resist. Grabbing him in her arms she gave him a giant hug, then explained.

As they were gathering up their cups, Joy asked the question she had been longing to ask but hadn't quite dared. "Terry, why don't you talk to Washington and your father?" She tried to appear nonchalant but she scarcely breathed, waiting for his answer.

Joy wasn't looking at Terry, but when he didn't answer, she turned and saw his blue eyes staring at her, sober and withdrawn for the first time today. When her eyes met his, he dropped his head.

Her heart quivered in alarm. Had she destroyed their rapport by prematurely questioning him?

Then his answer came, so low that she could hardly make out the words. "I-I can't talk to them." The words seemed wrung from him; his lips trembled, and each word seemed drenched with desperate misery.

"Why, Terry? Why can't you talk to them?" She longed to say more but was fearful of saying the wrong thing. Tension hung in the air, as fragile and brittle as icicles.

For a long moment, Terry said nothing. Then slowly he lifted his head and looked at her with terror-filled eyes. "They'd find out. Don't you see?"

"They'd find out what, Terry?" Joy asked in bewilderment.

He dropped his head again and muttered, "I can't tell you."

Joy felt pity boil up in her throat, threatening to choke her. "Terry —" she laid her hand on his shoulder and was deeply disturbed to feel it trembling.

What was the boy afraid of? Terrified was a better word for what she read in his eyes.

"Terry —" she said, feeling for the right words. A silent prayer welled up in her heart that she wouldn't say the wrong thing. "Do you mean that you could talk to your father — and others — if you wanted to, but you're afraid to?"

Numbly, Terry nodded his head in the affirmative. He raised his eyes to hers again, and the anguish mirrored there wrung Joy's heart until she felt physical pain.

With a quick flick of pink tongue, he wet his dry lips nervously. His voice was flat and his eyes were almost glazed, as if he were recalling something that was more than he could bear. "A-after the c-crash, when Washington found me, I r-really couldn't t-talk. M-my throat was all tight and the-the words just wouldn't come out."

Terry was staring at her but his eyes held a faraway look in them, as if he were seeing again the trauma of that night. "Then — later — everyone was trying to get me to tell them about the-the c-crash. Daddy — Washington — the doctors — everybody!" His voice sunk to a moan of despair. "B-but I-I couldn't tell them! Then they would k-know!"

Joy took one of Terry's ice cold hands in

hers. "Terry, sometimes it helps to talk to someone. Bottling everything up inside makes you feel bad. Can't you tell me, Terry? What are you afraid for everyone to know?"

"Y-you would hate me, t-too!" Suddenly Terry crumpled and began to sob, heart-rending sobs of bitter anguish and despair.

Without even thinking about what she was doing, Joy gathered the shuddering child into her arms and began to rock him gently back and forth. "Terry, I would never hate you, no matter what you did," she soothed. His arms crept up about her neck, but he continued to cry heartbreakingly.

But strangely, the sobs were not the dreadful keening sounds that had first brought her to Terry's door. These were the sobs of a distressed little boy.

Washington suddenly appeared at the door, alarm written vividly on his countenance. Joy shook her head at him and he reluctantly withdrew. But not very far, Joy suspected.

She continued to rock Terry and slowly the sobs subsided. Then Terry sat up and drew away from Joy self-consciously.

He rubbed at his eyes with a balled fist. Not looking at her, he said in a stricken voice, "I-I guess you t-think I'm a b-baby."

"Not at all," Joy said gently. "I have a good cry now and then myself. Now," she said briskly, "would you like me to read to you a little more *Captains Courageous* before I go see how Carole is doing?"

"You can if you want to." But Terry's voice was indifferent and remote.

Joy read part of a chapter but she could see that his mind just wasn't on Harvey's problems. Terry obviously had greater ones.

Laying the book aside, Joy said, "I had better go down and see about my friend."

"Are you coming back for dinner?"

"Carole and I are having dinner with your father tonight. But I can come by and say goodnight afterward, if you like."

At the mention of Skye, Terry's face took on the appearance of a thunderhead. "I'll probably be asleep already," he said ungraciously.

"Then I'll say goodnight now," Joy said lightly and moved toward the door. "And Terry, remember, if you need me, my door won't be locked. Okay?"

"Okay," Terry answered sulkily.

Joy went out and closed the door. She suddenly felt extremely tired and very discouraged. What had she accomplished today toward helping Terry? Absolutely nothing!

And suddenly she was desperately lonely for Mitzi. *Dear sweet, obedient daughter,* she thought. *You have never given me anything but joy and happiness. Thank God for you!*

19

At dinner that night, Skye was everything a host should be — charming, entertaining and polite. Kim, immaculately dressed in white shirt, black bow tie and black trousers, served.

A large platter containing a tender standing-rib roast, surrounded by small, whole, parsley-sprinkled potatoes, orangy carrots, baby peas and small white onions held the place of honor on the table. Crispy fresh vegetables surrounded a bowl of thick, creamy dressing and the aroma of freshly baked sourdough rolls filled the air.

As the meal was about to begin, Washington brought champagne on ice and set it at Skye's elbow.

Skye's eyes were faintly derisive as they regarded Joy. "Are you still 'on the wagon' tonight or will you join Mrs. Loring and me in a glass of champagne?"

Before Joy could answer, Carole spoke

pleasantly but decisively, "No champagne for me. I don't drink, either."

Skye's right eyebrow rose. "Two lovely ladies — a blonde and a brunette — and they neither one drink. What are you? Not religious fanatics, surely?"

Joy felt the color rising in her cheeks. But Carole answered, "I'm guilty of being just that!"

Skye's eyes narrowed as they rested on Carole. "But why do you choose — that path — when you obviously have everything your heart desires?" His voice was genuinely puzzled.

Carole's well-formed lips curved into a smile. "You're right. I have always had everything money could buy. And what it couldn't buy, I usually could obtain by fluttering my eyelashes or dropping a few tears."

A flicker of pain crossed Carole's lovely face. "But it couldn't buy happiness or peace of mind. Eight months ago, David — my husband — was bordering on being an alcoholic and our marriage was coming apart at the seams." Her blue-black eyes suddenly misted and she said softly, "Then we met Jesus Christ. He turned our lives around and put our marriage back together again. That's why I'm a Christian."

Skye looked relieved. "Oh, well, I'm a Christian, too." He laughed shortly, "But I don't let it hamper my lifestyle."

Carole smiled. "That's what I said. But with God, salvation is a total commitment and Jesus is either Lord of all or not Lord at all. Believe me, I found that out the hard way."

The mocking light was back in Skye's eyes as they swung to Joy. "And you're a fanatic, too?"

Slight color stained Joy's cheeks but she said firmly, "If being a totally committed Christian is a fanatic, then, yes, I'm one, too."

"Well!" Skye said, "I guess I'm outnumbered so I'll forego the pleasure!" He summoned Kim. "Pour tea for the ladies and take the wine away." He turned back to his guests. "Now, let's get started on that roast before it gets cold."

Joy adroitly turned the conversation to Skye's work, and throughout the meal he regaled them with stories — several uproariously funny — of his experiences at digs in many parts of the world. Archaeology was his passion and both women were amazed at the change in his manner when he talked about it. The mockery and bitterness were forgotten and his face reflected his enthusiasm.

When the meal was finished, Joy said, "I've told Carole how well you play. Would you mind playing the piano for us?"

Skye grinned affably, "I'd be delighted — if Mrs. Loring will play, too."

As they walked into the adjoining drawing room, Prince rose from his rug near the fire. Skye, leading the way, stooped and spoke softly to him, stroking the powerful animal's head before going on to the piano. Prince sank back down on his rug by the fire, ignoring Carole and Joy.

Carole and Skye were accomplished pianists, and Joy sat back contentedly in a comfortable reclining loveseat to listen. Although she knew Carole's knee was still painful, it hindered her very little at the piano since it was her left knee.

While Skye was playing, Carole sat with Joy in the loveseat. Suddenly Joy whispered, "Don't look now, but I'm sure Terry is behind that curtain listening. I saw it move ever so slightly."

Carole whispered back excitedly a moment later, "You're right! I saw it quiver. And every once in a while, the curtain parts a tiny bit. I wish I could get a good look at your mystery boy!"

"He'd vanish like a vapor in the wind if

he knew he'd been seen," Joy whispered back.

At that moment, Skye called, "Mrs. Kyle — Joy — would you like to sing for us? I know you can do that, I've heard you."

Joy protested that she knew nothing except hymns but both Skye and Carole insisted. So Joy sang while Carole accompanied her on the piano. Her voice was not trained but it rang pure and clear as she sang the stirringly familiar, "How Great Thou Art."

Suddenly, Joy's heart leaped. For a brief moment, Terry's face and neck appeared where the curtain came together. He had apparently become absorbed in the singing and forgotten himself. His blue eyes, fixed on her face as she sang, were big and luminous.

Then Skye shifted his position where he was leaning on the edge of the piano and instantly Terry vanished.

When Joy had finished the song, Skye, without a word, walked across to the heavy curtain and drew it aside. The narrow passageway behind it was empty. Slowly he drew the drapery back across the opening and returned to the piano.

His face was inscrutable as he looked at

Joy. "We had a visitor again."

"I know," Joy acknowledged.

Skye lowered his voice. "Did you find out anything this afternoon? Washington said the boy was crying at one point."

"Not as much as I would have liked. Terry seems to feel he has done something terrible — that's why he was crying. He's convinced everyone will hate him if they find out what he did."

"Hate him? Terry was a little mischievous sometimes but. . . ."

"Whatever it was seems to be connected with the airplane crash and his mother."

"You couldn't get him to tell you anything about what this horrible act was?"

"Not a word. He said I would hate him if I knew. That's when he cried Whether this deed he is afraid for anyone to find out about is real or imaginary, it is extremely real to him."

"Would he talk to you about the airplane accident?"

Joy shook her head. "I didn't really press him to talk about it. He seems fearful of revealing his terrible deed if he talks about the plane crash."

Shaking his head, Skye said warmly, "I do appreciate the effort you are making to help Terry."

"I like Terry," Joy said, "so it is my pleasure. I just hope I can discover something that will help."

"You've already discovered more than all of the expensive doctors."

Joy laughed lightly. "I have one advantage. I look like his mother."

Skye was watching her with an odd, scrutinizing, almost puzzled look. "Yes," he said slowly, "the hair and eyes and even your build is similar but . . ." he broke off and turned away.

Somewhat subdued, Joy said, "Well, I'm feeling pretty tired. I think I'll go upstairs."

"Me, too," added Carole, reaching for her crutches. "But it was an enjoyable evening. If only David —" Carole stopped abruptly and smiled wistfully. "I know David, my husband, would have enjoyed it, too."

Nodding distractedly, Skye muttered a brief acknowledgment and said good night.

Joy considered going to Terry's room to say good night after they left Skye but decided against it. If he wanted — or needed — to see her, he had only to come to her room.

Carole was quiet after they returned to their room and began to prepare for bed. From her comments Joy knew she missed her husband.

186

If I ever marry again, I hope my husband is as loving and thoughtful as David, she thought as she slipped into bed and turned out the bedside light. An image of Jeffrey Pitman crossed her mind. He appeared to be the same dependable, sweet, kind and thoughtful type of man as David. *Besides, he seems to really care about me,* she mused.

Unbidden, her thoughts jumped to Skye Windthorn. What a paradox he was! He could be kind and gentle and entertaining. Then in a flash he was arrogant, sarcastic, mocking — and seething with bitterness and resentment! Pity the poor girl who married him! Strangely, thoughts of Jeffrey caused not a ripple in her heart, but thoughts of Skye sent a strange excitement coursing through her veins.

"Dear God," her whispered prayer was a desperate plea, "Please don't let me make a mistake again!" A new realization sprang into her mind. Skye Windthorn was not about to fall in love with a girl who resembled his unfaithful dead wife. She was in no danger of marrying Skye! Oddly, the thought didn't bring the relief it should have.

20

Joy was still awake a half hour later when she heard the soft swish of her door opening. Her heart began to thump and she strained to see in the dark shadows near the door.

Then the small figure of Terry Windthorn appeared in the dim glow of her nightlight. She could see the gleam of his eyes and the pathetic thinness of his pajamaed form as he advanced noiselessly to her bedside.

"I'm awake, Terry," Joy said softly. "Do you need something?"

She could hear Terry's rapid breathing, now — as if he had been running.

She raised up in the bed alarmed. "Is something wrong, Terry?"

"N-no, I-I . . ." he gulped in a deep breath, "It just scares me to be out of my room. So I-I ran down the hall."

"Were you afraid a while ago — behind

the curtain in the drawing room?" Joy asked.

"Not after I got there," Terry said frankly. "If you're there, I'm not afraid. But I had to run all the way there and back, I was so scared."

"What are you afraid of?"

"I don't know. But my heart beats real hard; my throat gets tight and dry — like chalk — and I can hardly breathe. It's like — like something is going to get me — or-or something terrible is going to happen every time I go out of my room."

"Jesus doesn't want you to be afraid."

There was a pause, as if Terry was considering that, then he spoke matter-of-factly, "Jesus doesn't like me."

Shocked, Joy said quickly, "That's not true! Of course, Jesus likes you. He loves you!"

"Doesn't Jesus know everything?" Terry asked quickly.

"Yes."

"Then He knows what I did! So He doesn't like me, either."

Joy sprang out of bed, drew her robe about her, and stuck her feet into scuffs. Switching on her lamp, she said determinedly, "Terry, sit down. We need to talk."

She saw that Terry had backed away to-

ward the door. His eyes mirrored alarm —
and a certain wariness.

Joy dropped down on a small sofa and
patted the place beside her. "Come on and
sit down," she said softly. "I'm not going to
make you tell anything you don't want to
tell." When he still looked doubtful, she
smiled entreatingly, "I promise."

Terry came slowly, his eyes still upon
her, and perched on a padded footstool
near her.

"Now, Terry, let me repeat first of all
that Jesus does not want you to be afraid.
Over and over in the Bible He told His
people not to be afraid. Have you ever invited Jesus into your heart?"

Terry stared at her, obviously not understanding what she meant. "I didn't know I
was supposed to."

"You know Jesus came into the world as
a little baby, don't you?"

Terry grinned faintly. "The Christmas
story."

"Right! Jesus was God's Son but He
came to the earth as a little baby and grew
up and died on a cross to pay for my sins
and your sins. But He didn't stay dead. He
rose again and because He lives, we can
live forever. Do you know what sins are?"

"Bad things?"

"Yes, the bad things that we all have done. We ask God to forgive us for those bad things and tell Him we believe Jesus died to pay for them and rose from the dead. If we ask Jesus to come into our hearts and be our Lord, then His Spirit comes to live in our hearts. And with Jesus in our hearts, we don't have to be afraid. Do you understand?"

Terry bent his head and for a long moment, he said nothing. Then he looked up quizzically, "You mean I can ask God to forgive me for that awful thing I did, and He won't be mad at me anymore for doing it?"

"That's right. In fact, the Bible says that God will throw our sins away and never remember them again. Then it's like we never did them. Would you like God to forgive that big old thing you did and then toss it away forever, Terry?"

Joy could see the struggle going on in Terry's mind registered on his face. Hope glimmered in his eyes, but doubt that God would really forgive his horrendous act, also wavered there. "Are you s-sure God would f-forgive me? Would He like me, then?"

Pity surged up into Joy's breast in a suffocating wave. No wonder this poor child was tormented with fears of all kinds. To

191

believe that God disliked him was a terrible and overwhelming load for his frail shoulders to carry!

"I can prove it," Joy said emphatically. "Jesus loved us all so much that He gave His life to pay for our sins. If you died for someone, that must mean you love them better than your own life. Isn't that so?"

Suddenly Terry's face lit up like a floodlight had switched on inside his head. "I believe you!" The light seemed to dim abruptly. "But I don't know how to talk to God. What do I say?"

"You talk to God just like anyone else. Let me pray first and then you can pray. I'll help you if you want me to."

Joy took one of Terry's small, thin hands in both her warm ones, bowed her head and closed her eyes.

"Dear heavenly Father, thank you for sending your son, Jesus, to die for our sins. Thank you for loving us. Please, forgive Terry Windthorn for all his sins and wash his heart clean. Dear Jesus, come into his heart and live there and take away his fears and help him to live for you. In your name, amen."

Joy waited a minute but Terry said nothing. She opened her eyes to find him staring at her. "Would you like me to pray and you repeat the words after me?" she said gently.

"D-do I have to say out loud what I did?" Terry asked in a worried tone.

"Of course not! God already knows anyway."

Terry breathed a sigh of relief, closed his eyes and began falteringly, "Dear God, y-you know what I d-did." His voice quivered and then steadied. "I-I'm awful sorry. You know I am, don't you? P-please forgive me for doing that and for all the other bad things. And please, God, would you forget I did 'em like Joy said you would?"

He paused and then spoke more easily. "And I need Jesus to come and live in my heart 'cause I get awful scared lots of time. That's all, I guess, except — thanks. Amen."

Terry raised his head and asked anxiously, "Do you think He really will forgive me?"

"Did you mean it when you said you were sorry?"

Terry nodded his head up and down vigorously.

"Then God not only will, but He already has forgiven you!"

Slow wonder seemed to dawn in Terry's eyes.

"Now," Joy said, "you had better get to bed. If Washington finds you gone, he will be worried and come looking for you."

Sudden fear loomed in Terry's eyes. "I-I don't like that dark hall. Will you go with me? That Midnight Cat Burglar might be out there."

Joy drew in her breath sharply. "Who told you about the cat burglar?"

"Kim did. He said he climbs up the wall like a spider and creeps into houses when it gets dark." Terry shivered.

"Even a cat burglar wouldn't be out in a storm like this," Joy said emphatically. She was extremely annoyed that Kim had told the child about the burglar. No wonder Terry was afraid to leave his room at night.

Joy took Terry to his room and tucked him in bed. She offered to stay until he was asleep but once in his room, his fear vanished.

"There are a couple of verses from the Bible that will help you not to be afraid, even in the dark hall," Joy told him before she left. "Just repeat it when you are afraid and you'll remember that Jesus is with you. 'Do not fear, for I am with you.' And Jesus said, 'Lo, I am with you always.'"

Terry repeated the words a couple of times to plant them in his mind. Joy then kissed him lightly on the cheek, softly said goodnight, turned off the light and went out into the hall.

She had just passed the last door before turning the corner to the corridor leading to her room when she heard a low growl. The door swung open noiselessly and Prince's dark figure advanced, barring her way.

Joy froze. She could see the gleam of his dark eyes and the white of his teeth in the dim hall light. Fear rose in her throat and her legs felt like soft butter. "Dear God, help *me*," she breathed.

Suddenly a light flashed on inside and a voice spoke sharply, "Here, Prince!"

Prince slipped back into the doorway without another glance at her. Joy took a tentative step forward to see if her shaky legs would carry her. She heard the faint squeak of floorboards, then Skye was standing in the door, tying the belt of his bathrobe.

"I-I just took Terry back to his room," Joy hastened to explain. "He came to my room and. . . ."

"Is he okay?"

"Perfectly. I suppose he was just lonely. I'm sorry I woke you. Goodnight." Joy moved quickly away down the hall before

Skye could question her further. She wasn't sure Skye would be pleased that she had talked to Terry about God.

Although he didn't detain her, she felt Skye's eyes following her as she rounded the corner, but she didn't look back.

21

Joy lay awake for a long while, too restless to sleep. She was not so naive as to expect that all of Terry's problems would immediately vanish, but having Christ in his life was a big start.

I wonder if Terry really has done something terrible, or if it's a tiny thing that has become a mountain in his mind? she mused. A little chill crept down her backbone. What if he *had* done something horrible? He was an intelligent child. Wouldn't he know the difference between something really bad and something insignificant?

What horrendous thing could a child do when he was only five-years-old, though? Something so awful that three years later he still could not bear to talk about it. She pondered. Steal something of immense value? Perhaps. But that wouldn't be so terrible that a child would be convinced God hated him for his crime, would it? But one never knew the thoughts of a child. A child's values were not the same as an adult's.

However, the deed seemed to be directly connected with the plane crash that had killed Terry's mother and Skye's best friend. Did the child blame himself because he had lived and his idolized mother had died? No, that didn't make sense. Terry had thought his crime so great that God could never forgive him.

There I go again, using the word "crime," she thought, *as if any act of a five-year-old could be that serious! Preposterous!*

She tried to will herself to forget the problem of Terry's real or imaginary deed and go to sleep, but she kept seeing the boy's wretched face. She could only imagine how horrible it would be for a child to carry around the load of guilt Terry had carried for three years.

As she tried to think through the problem, she recalled Skye saying that Terry would seem happy enough at times and then would drop back into a brooding, listless state, not eating, and disinterested in everything. That would explain why he was little more than skin and bones.

If only Terry would tell her about this monstrous thing that was tearing him apart! Perhaps she could help. Surely someone could. Even to share the awful secret would help him.

"Father God," she prayed softly, "help Terry realize he needs to share his fear of what he has done with me or someone who can help." As Joy finally drifted off to sleep, she committed Terry's problems to God.

Quite a while later she awoke with a start. Something had lightly touched her face! Opening her eyes, she saw bright sunlight shining into the room and Terry standing beside her bed.

She reached for her robe and swung her feet to the floor. "You rascalatious kid! Why did you wake me up?" she grumbled teasingly.

But Terry would not be daunted today. "I walked down to your room and wasn't afraid," he exulted. "Well, I was a little at first," he admitted, "but I said those verses all the way down here and — here I am!"

"That's just great!" Joy was fully awake now. "What time is it?"

"Ten o'clock. I had breakfast hours ago. I thought you were never going to wake up."

Suddenly a voice called from the next room, "Are you finally awake, Joy?" There was the sound of a few quick taps and

Carole stood in the doorway between their rooms. "See, I'm improving. Just one crutch today! I . . ." She stopped abruptly when she saw Terry.

Joy had seen fear leap into Terry's eyes when Carole first called. Now as she entered the room, he made a wild dash for the door.

Joy rushed after him and caught his hand before he could go fleeing down the hall. "Terry, please wait."

Joy placed both hands on Terry's trembling shoulders and forced him to look at her. "Terry, Jesus does not want you to be afraid! Remember how He helped you just now? When you were afraid in the hall, you just repeated Jesus' promise from the Bible that He is with you all the time."

The child's eyes were fixed on her face, but she could feel the tremors shaking his thin body. His eyes were enormous blue pools of desperate fear.

"Terry, this is my friend, Carole. She won't hurt you. And she loves Jesus as much as you and I do."

Quickly grasping the situation, Carole stood unmoving in the doorway.

Terry darted a quick, wild-eyed glance at Carole and then back to Joy. She smiled at him. He looked back at Carole. She also smiled but made no move toward him.

Joy saw his lips move and caught the faint words, "Do not fear . . . I am with you always." He repeated the words slowly, almost inaudibly, three times as they waited silently. The terror slowly receded from his face and the trembling diminished.

Finally, Terry heaved a big sigh and said somewhat tremulously to Joy, "J-Jesus helped me again, didn't He?"

"Yes, Terry, and He always will because He loves you. And Jesus always keeps His promises. Now, would you like to say hello to my friend, Carole?"

Terry gulped and then said shyly, "H-Hello, Carole."

"Hello, Terry," Carole's smile brought a dimple into one smooth cheek. Her blue-black eyes sparkled with warmth. "Kim just brought in breakfast for Joy and me. Will you join us? There's plenty."

"I-I already ate."

"Surely you can drink some hot chocolate and eat one of those delicious croissants," Carole urged.

"Umm. That does sound good," Joy said. "I think I'm ready for them. Terry, if you had breakfast a long time ago, we can ring Washington for some lunch for you. How about it?"

"Okay," Terry agreed reluctantly, following them into Carole's room.

But a few minutes later when Washington brought a ham omelet with sliced, ripe tomatoes and a large glass of milk, Terry sat down and ate the whole meal.

While they were eating, Joy told Carole about Terry's large library. Books were a safe topic to discuss with Terry, and although the boy said only a few words here and there, they were able to draw him into the conversation.

After Terry went back to his room for his lessons, Joy went to her room to dress. As she entered the room, she drew in her breath sharply. The waterfall picture was back in its place on her wall!

Although the picture being taken out and returned troubled her, she rationalized that it had no doubt just been taken down for repairs. But it worried her that whoever kept moving it was so secretive. *I suppose they really aren't,* she decided. *They just happen to come when I'm out. I'm edgy, I guess.*

Her thoughts were interrupted by a knock at the door. Kim had a message for Joy. "When it is convenient, Mr. Windthorn would like to see you in his study."

"Tell him I'll come down as soon as I'm dressed," Joy said.

A few minutes later, Joy tapped on the study door.

She went in at Skye's call to enter. He was sitting at a massive oak desk on which were spread an assortment of large books, obviously reference books, as well as the closed case that housed the ancient leather scroll he was deciphering.

Prince was reclining on a rug near the fireplace where a log sent its spluttering, crackling warmth into the room. He opened sleepy eyes to look at Joy indifferently, stretched — showing powerful, rippling muscles — and yawned luxuriously before settling back down.

Skye rose with a smile on his lean face and said pleasantly, "Sit there by the fire." He indicated a large leather chair and sat down in its counterpart across from her.

Joy spread her hands to the warmth of the blazing log. "There is nothing more pleasurable than a wood fire when it's cold and snowy outdoors."

"I agree," Skye said. "How is Mrs. Loring this morning?"

"Much better. She is only using one crutch now and has almost no pain as long as she doesn't move her knee too much."

"Good!" Skye hesitated. "Washington tells me that Terry not only ate a very hearty breakfast but that he also ate with you and Mrs. Loring. That's an amazing development. Terry has always been terrified of strangers."

"I know. He had come down to see me and he almost bolted from the room when Carole appeared. So I thought he had made remarkable progress when he agreed to have breakfast with us." Joy quickly decided that it might be better not to tell Terry's father that he had defeated his fear by relying on God. That could come later.

Skye's grey eyes were warm with approval. "I am simply astounded at the improvement in the boy since you have been working with him." He made a wry face. "As you probably are aware, I haven't wanted a woman in the house because of my personal aversion to them. But if I had known the beneficial effects one could have on Terry, I would have tried this long ago."

"I'm still concerned about the horrible thing that Terry is convinced he has done," Joy said thoughtfully. "You don't have any idea of what it might be?"

"Not the foggiest! But surely a five-year-old couldn't have done anything too terrible."

"That's what I was thinking. But

whether Terry actually did something horrendous or not, he is convinced he did. I'm sure it would help if he would tell someone about it."

Skye's laugh was bitter. "Remember, he hasn't talked to me — or anyone else, for that matter — since his mother died . . . until you came." A strange expression crept into his eyes. "It's so odd that he talked to you."

Skye's face suddenly hardened and his eyes went bleak, but he spoke softly, "Has that boy been deceiving all of us? Could he have talked all along if he had wanted to?"

Joy swallowed hard. She had to answer truthfully — but could she make Terry's father understand?

Seeing her hesitation, Skye leaned toward Joy, his voice deadly quiet. "He *could* have talked all along! It's written in your face! That little scoundrel!"

"No, wait!" Joy cried out. "It isn't like it sounds. Please let me explain."

"Please do," Skye said sarcastically.

Joy looked into those flinty grey eyes and stern face and suddenly was almost tongue-tied. Skye Windthorn was again the intimidating man she had first known. *No wonder his son is afraid to tell him anything,* she thought.

"T-Terry told me that when Washington found him at the site of the airplane crash, he really couldn't talk. He said his throat just seemed to close up and he couldn't speak. Later, he was afraid to speak because everyone kept asking him about the crash and he couldn't talk about it or you would have found out what he had done."

Skye looked incredulous. "But that doesn't make sense!"

"To a child it could make very good sense."

"I don't believe that rot about being afraid to talk," Skye said savagely.

"But why would he lie about something like that?" Joy reasoned. "There had to be a reason for him to just suddenly stop talking."

"You said Terry was angry with me for making his mother cry," Skye said. "I think he just wanted to punish me for what he feels I did to his mother!" His voice had grown cold and harsh.

"I don't believe that!" Joy said, shock registering in her voice. "Perhaps the awful deed he believes he did has grown all out of proportion, but I believe the weight of guilt he has carried caused his fears and . . ."

"And I still believe the little scamp made

up the whole story — he's a sharp boy, you know. A supposedly horrible crime — one so awful that he is afraid to talk about it. Hmph! No wonder he's afraid to talk about it! There isn't anything to tell!"

Joy was speechless with horror.

"And, I also believe the boy's vindictive little plot to punish his father backfired. He didn't know how to stop the malicious little game and it has nearly made a nervous wreck out of him, trying to keep up the charade."

"You don't really believe a five-year-old is capable of planning such a diabolical thing?" Joy asked, appalled.

"He confessed to you that he could have talked all along if he had wanted to, didn't he? If he was capable of deceiving us all — doctors, nurses — even Washington, who has cared for him like a mother — wouldn't he be capable of deceiving you about a terrible crime that he supposedly perpetrated?"

Joy could only shake her head in disbelief.

Skye laughed suddenly, a bark of derision. "His mother deceived me; now her son has deceived me. And to think that I have been practically bankrupting myself trying to help that boy! Flying in every specialist that anyone recommended and paying their outlandish fees!"

Skye's shoulders suddenly slumped and he said, almost as if to himself, "When I told Lillian that I couldn't even be sure Terry was mine, I was probably right. I have had the responsibility of a child who isn't even mine and he repays me this way!"

"You don't know Terry isn't your own son," Joy cried out in dismay. "All of this is conjecture. You have nothing to substantiate your accusations against either your wife or Terry! Besides, you're all he has whether he's your natural son or not!" Suddenly, to her horror, she burst into tears.

Humiliated, and angry at herself — and Skye — for her outburst, Joy jumped to her feet and hurried toward the door.

22

Before Joy got halfway to the door, Skye caught and stopped her with a strong hand on her arm. "I'm sorry, Joy. I didn't mean to make you cry." He handed her a large white handkerchief from his pocket. "Please come back and sit down." He sounded truly contrite.

Feeling somewhat foolish, Joy let Skye guide her back to her chair. By the time she was seated again, Joy had composed herself.

"Maybe I am jumping to a lot of hasty conclusions," Skye said. "Perhaps it would be wise to have Washington bring Terry down and see if we can make some sense out of all this."

"Y-you mean try to get Terry to tell us what he is afraid of?"

"Certainly! Why not?"

"I don't think that's a good idea," Joy said slowly.

"Why not?" Skye repeated brusquely.

"Terry is making marvelous improvement, but if we begin to push him into what he isn't ready for, we may lose all the ground we have gained."

"But if he is deceiving us all, the quicker he knows we are on to his tricks, the sooner . . ."

"I still don't believe Terry is lying," Joy interrupted, "but if he were, I think it just shows he needs patience and understanding. Couldn't I work with him a bit more first and see what I can do with him?"

Skye began to pace back and forth in the room, a frown knotting his face. Joy watched him uneasily. Finally Skye came and stood before her. "I have been soft and lenient with Terry long enough and see what it has gotten me? Absolutely nowhere! I honestly cannot see that it will hurt to talk to Terry."

"Oh, please don't!" Joy said anxiously.

But Skye's jaw firmed into an implacable, stubborn line and she knew it would do no good to plead further.

Washington came quickly in response to Skye's ring. When Skye requested him to bring Terry down, Washington stood for a moment before he spoke, "Begging your pardon, sir, but I think you would have

better results with Terry if you go to his
room. You know how unhappy he is away
from it. We certainly don't want to bring
on one of those wailing spells."

"Do as I ask, Washington," Skye said impatiently.

"Very well, sir," Washington was cour-
teous but unsmiling.

As they waited for Terry, Skye sat staring
broodingly into the fire. Joy longed to
plead with that formidable, stony face to
be gentle with Terry because he was only a
small boy. But the words died before she
could birth them. After all, Terry was not
her son and she had no right to tell Skye
how to deal with the boy.

When Washington led Terry into the
room, Joy felt her heart constrict with pity.
Terry's face was pasty white and his eyes
were wide with anxiety. Washington hesitated as if he would like to stay but Skye
dismissed him almost curtly.

When Terry's eyes sought hers, Joy tried
to smile as warmly as she could.

"Sit down, Terry." Skye's voice was unemotional, but not unkind.

Terry perched himself in a large leather
chair. The huge chair dwarfed him, making
him look even more frail and defenseless
than usual.

Skye took a chair facing Terry. After a moment, he leaned toward the child. "Terry, Mrs. Kyle tells me you can talk. That you could have talked the past three years if you had wanted to."

Terry's eyes darted to Joy's face and the agonized look of betrayal on his face brought an exclamation to Joy's lips. "Terry, Mr. Windthorn is your father! I-I had no choice."

Terry dropped his eyes but not before she saw the wary, guarded expression that sprang into them. The child waited silently.

Just waiting for the axe to fall, Joy thought bitterly. Suddenly she almost disliked Skye. *Whoa, Joy,* she cautioned herself sternly. *This is not your child and you have no right to interfere. Besides, you don't really know how Skye will handle this.*

Skye cleared his throat. "I'm waiting for your explanation, Terry." His voice was still flat, devoid of emotion. "Mrs. Kyle feels you had good reason for hiding from us the fact that you could talk."

Terry still sat very still, not raising his head. His agitation showed only in the pallor of his skin and the white knuckles of the hands that gripped the arms of his chair.

After a moment Skye spoke again. A trace of impatience had crept into his voice. "I'm not scolding you, Terry, I'm just asking for an explanation."

Suddenly Joy couldn't stand anymore. "Terry," she implored, "Please tell your father what you told me! Please!"

He slowly lifted his head, his blue eyes empty and hopeless. When he spoke, his voice was low but as even as his father's, and just as unemotional. He didn't look at either Skye or Joy but stared into the fire. "Where do you want me to start?"

Skye gave a visible start when Terry spoke and Joy recalled that Skye had not heard him speak for three years.

"I would like to hear what happened the evening of the crash," Skye said.

Joy held her breath. Would Terry tell his fearsome secret?

For a long moment, Terry continued to stare into the fire. Then he flicked a glance at his father, and back to the blazing log. His low voice sounded weary and resigned. "I heard you and Mamma quarreling. When she ran out of the room crying, I went to my room. It hurt me to see her cry."

Skye made an impatient gesture but if Terry noticed he gave no indication.

"I stayed in my room the rest of the evening. Washington brought my supper. Mamma always came to tuck me in but that night she didn't come for a long time.

"I had gone to sleep, but Mamma woke me up kissing me good night. I hugged her and her breath smelled bad — kinda sour, like it did when she drank too much wine. She held me so tight that I cried out. Then she let me go and said something like, 'I'll come back to see you. I promise, Baby.' Then she hugged and kissed me again and went out the door."

Skye was watching Terry as if in a trance.

Terry seemed to have forgotten anyone else was there. His voice quickened, "For a little bit I didn't know what Mamma had meant. Then suddenly I knew! She was leaving me. I was scared. Mamma couldn't leave without me!

"I jumped up quick, put on my bathrobe, grabbed Sparky and ran out into the hall. Mamma was gone. I ran down the hall to her room but she wasn't there. Then I ran into Daddy's room. Mamma wasn't there but there was a piece of paper on his pillow."

Skye's dark eyes were intent on Terry's face and his hands were clenched tightly in fists.

"I got the paper and ran out of the room fast, down the back stairs and outside. I knew if Mamma was leaving, she might be going in Daddy's plane because Bob had already taken her up once that day."

Skye made a slightly strangled sound but Terry went on almost hypnotically.

"When I got outside, I could hear the plane. I ran as fast as I could toward the runway. . . ."

Suddenly Skye spoke. "Terry, what did you do with the note that Lillian left for me on my pillow?" His voice was taut with strain.

Terry turned his eyes slowly to look at his father. When he didn't answer for a moment, Skye spoke again, sharply, "The note your mother left for me! What did you do with it?"

Skye loved his wife deeply, Joy thought in amazement. *Even now, a note from her unfaithful grave means a lot to him.*

Terry seemed to come back to reality with a snap. "The note? What note?" His face wore a blank look.

"The note you said Lillian left for me — on my pillow. Where did it go? You said you took it."

"I-I don't know. I had forgotten about it until just now," the boy said slowly.

215

"Think, Terry," Skye's eyes bored into Terry's.

The boy drew back fearfully, and his eyes slid away. "I-I don't remember what I did with the note." A frown furrowed his forehead. "Let's see, I grabbed it and ran down the back stairs." His lips trembled as he turned back to his father, "Honest, I can't remember anything else about it."

"Maybe you put it in your pocket or placed it in a drawer or somewhere else before you left the room," suggested his father.

Terry shook his head slowly, "I-I don't know. I can't remember what I did with it."

"What did you take the note for in the first place?" Skye's voice had roughened.

Terry's eyes wore a desperate look. "I d-don't know why I took it. I-I guess I wasn't thinking right."

"You most certainly weren't! Taking something that did not belong to you!" Skye was glaring at Terry now.

The boy cowered down in the huge leather seat and dropped his eyes.

"Mr. Windthorn," Joy implored, "you can't blame Terry for losing the note. He was extremely upset about his mother leaving. Besides, he was only five-years-old at the time and it's been three years!"

Skye turned dark, stern eyes upon Joy and said coldly, "Please, stay out of this, Mrs. Kyle."

He turned back to Terry and said scathingly, "Maybe there wasn't a note! You lied to me about not being able to talk. Maybe there never was a note!"

Joy gasped and protested, "How can you say such a thing?"

Skye ignored her. "And what about this deep, dark secret that you were afraid for anyone to find out about?" His voice was harsh and cutting. "That was a lie, too, wasn't it? Something you told the pretty lady to get her sympathy!"

Abruptly he stood to his feet and started to turn away from them. His hand struck the thin scroll case and it fell to the floor. With a violent oath, Skye bent to pick it up and stopped in midair.

Joy heard his strangled exclamation and saw his face go ashy-white. He stood as if petrified. She moved quickly to the end of the desk and looked down. The scroll case was lying open on the floor, but for a few seconds Joy didn't comprehend why Skye was almost in a state of shock. Then it hit her. The case was empty!

Skye stooped and lifted the case, setting it on the desk. "It can't be gone," he said in a low, agitated voice. "I put the scroll back in the case last night." He looked up at Joy but he wasn't seeing her, she knew. "I haven't had the case open this morning."

"Did you lock it into your desk?" Joy asked.

Skye looked at her for a moment as if he didn't understand what she was saying, then he said testily, "Of course I did! As soon as I finish with the scroll for the day I always put it back in the case and place it in a locked drawer of my desk."

"Maybe Washington or Kim know something about it," Joy suggested. "After all, it couldn't have just walked off."

Without a word, Skye pressed a buzzer on his desk and Washington was at the door within a couple of minutes. In the meantime, Skye quickly searched the drawers of his desk.

When Skye told him of the missing scroll, Washington exclaimed in astonishment, "But how could it be gone, sir? You know neither Kim nor I ever touch it. We have our orders!"

Skye said nothing but pressed the buzzer on his desk twice. Kim knocked on the door almost immediately.

He seemed as shocked as Washington when Skye informed him that the scroll was gone, and declared that he had not seen it.

"Are you sure you put the scroll back in the case, sir?" Washington asked.

"Positive," Skye said emphatically. "That document is irreplaceable, extremely valuable. I carefully put it back in the case and lock it in my desk each time I leave this room."

His dark eyes swept the room. "Someone in this house took that scroll." His voice was harsh and angry.

"Maybe the Midnight Cat Burglar got in and stole it," Terry said suddenly into the tense silence.

"In this storm?" Skye's voice was scornful.

Suddenly a thought flashed into Joy's mind and she blurted it out. "The picture in my room. Could it be hidden there?"

Skye looked at her as if she had just taken leave of her senses. "What picture? What are you talking about?"

Joy quickly told him about the picture disappearing from her room and then reappearing this morning.

Skye's dark eyes were inscrutable as he said quietly, "Let's go see." He led the way out into the hall, with Washington, Kim and Joy following.

Joy saw that Terry made no move to go with them. Except for his suggestion about the cat burglar, he had sat unmoving and watchful during the excitement.

Skye stepped back to the door. "You come, too, Terry."

Terry came, but with lagging steps.

23

They entered Joy's room. Skye strode purposefully to the waterfall picture and took it off the wall. Laying it face down on the floor, he took a small knife from his pocket and began to carefully pry out the little metal diamonds holding the picture in place.

Suddenly Carole called, "Joy, are you in there?"

"Yes, come on in."

They heard the thump of crutches and Carole came swinging into the room through the small adjoining hall. In a few swift words, Joy told her about the missing scroll.

Skye had removed all the metal brads now and was carefully raising the heavy cardboard backing. Joy could feel the tension in the room as each one leaned forward to see.

Everyone but Terry.

Joy noticed that he stood just inside the

door, seemingly disinterested and detached from the adult concern. With a sinking feeling starting in the pit of her stomach, Joy wondered if he had stolen the scroll. Then her attention was drawn back to Skye as he lifted the back from the picture.

There was nothing there.

Joy felt foolish. "Well, even if the scroll isn't in the picture, someone took that picture away and later returned it," she defended herself.

Skye ignored her words. He laid the cardboard back on the picture and rose dispiritedly. His dark eyes, smoldering with anger, swept the assembled group. "One of you in this room stole that scroll! I want to know who!"

His scorching gaze riveted upon each one in turn, probing and accusing. When his eyes focused on her, Joy felt her heart give a lurch and it took all the courage she could muster to meet that condemning glare unflinchingly. Carole's eyes were icicle cool as they met Skye's stern, hot glare. No one but Terry failed to meet Skye's gaze, and he didn't even look up.

"We have been snowbound for the last four days. The scroll has disappeared in the last twelve hours. I think the conclusion is obvious. I will leave one last thought with each of you. If that scroll appears back on my desk in the next twenty-four hours, I'll not try to find out who took it." His hard eyes raked each one briefly, then he said, "Kim, please put that picture back together and rehang it."

"Okay, boss," Kim said quickly, "as soon as I get some tools." He left the room with rapid strides.

Washington moved out of the door with Terry ahead of him. "Terry," Skye called, "we still need to finish our talk." He turned to Joy. "And I would like you to come back to my office, also, if you would." His tone was polite and distant. He stalked off down the hall.

Joy walked silently beside Terry whose slumped figure looked like he was going to the gallows. Unwillingly, her thoughts taunted her with one question. Had Terry — for some strange reason of his own, maybe even to spite his father — taken the scroll? She hoped fervently that he had not!

Skye was waiting at the door of the study when she and Terry reached it. They entered and he closed the door.

Joy got one glimpse of Terry's blue eyes as he slid into a huge leather chair. She had seen the same trapped and frightened look on caged animals.

Joy sat down, too, but Skye remained standing. He paced the length of the room twice before he stopped in front of Terry. When he spoke, it was in a forced, flat voice. "Terry, did you take that scroll?"

When the boy did not answer, he said patiently, "That scroll is very valuable and it was entrusted to me. If I don't find it, I may be in a lot of trouble. Do you understand?"

"I didn't take it." His words were low, and Terry didn't look up.

"Terry, look at me." Skye's voice was deadly calm.

Terry reluctantly raised his head.

"Terry, you did take the scroll, didn't you? I won't punish you, if you will go and get it and bring it to me now."

From where she was sitting Joy could see Terry's face clearly. She saw tears well up in his eyes, and he said in a choking voice, "Why do you think I took it? I never! I told you, I didn't take it. Why don't you believe me?"

Skye's face hardened and his voice was sharp. "You lied to me about not being able to speak. If you would lie about that, you could be lying about this, too."

Terry hung his head and muttered, "But I didn't steal it."

"What about the marble statue that you took from my desk?"

Terry's head came up in surprise. "I didn't take that statue!"

"Don't deny it, Terry," Skye said impatiently. "Washington found it in your room two times."

Terry dropped his head and muttered sullenly, "I don't care. I didn't take it."

Skye took a deep breath as if struggling to remain calm. "Let's just forget about the paperweight. It isn't important but the scroll is — very, very important, Terry. If I don't find it, I could be in extremely bad trouble. Please get it for me, Terry. Right now!"

Tears were running down Terry's face as he met his father's gaze. But Skye seemed unaware of them. Terry's voice shook as he repeated, "I didn't take it, honest, I didn't."

"What makes you think Terry took it?" Joy broke in. "Maybe one of your servants stole it."

Skye turned cold eyes upon Joy. "Washington or Kim?" His laugh was derisive. "Washington has been with our family since I was a baby except for a couple of years when he served in the Korean war as a medic. I would trust him with my life.

"And Kim was a homeless waif on the streets of Hawaii when I brought him home with me six years ago! He has paid me back with absolute loyalty and perfect service! Kim hardly ever leaves the house except to ski or for an occasional date with a girl down at the resort on his day off. How could he even meet someone to whom he could sell a rare scroll such as this?"

His eyes narrowed, "I would think you or your friend took it but I know you both have access to fortunes. That leaves only Terry." He turned back toward his son, his voice scornful and derisive. "A son who is as deceitful as his two-timing mother."

Suddenly the small boy leaped from the huge chair, erupting into a boiling caldron of outrage. "How dare you talk about my mother that way!" The voice that crackled into the room was high, shrill and bordered on hysteria. Two spots of red burned in the child's white cheeks and his blue eyes were wild and glassy.

Joy sat petrified with shock. Skye took a step backward, stunned and incredulous. Terry looked every inch his father's son as he stood facing Skye, scorn and fury clearly etched in every line of his small body.

"Mamma loved me and you never did!" Terry shouted at his father. His mouth twisted as if in pain. "You said I wasn't even your son! Well, I don't want to be your son! I hate you!"

"Terry!" Skye's voice held deadly menace. "Shut your mouth before I . . ."

"I won't!" Terry screamed in fury. "You made my mother cry — and — and called her bad names! I hate you — I hate you — I hate you!"

"Go to your room, before I do something I'll be sorry for." Skye's face was almost as white as his son's and his voice trembled with rage.

"Please go, Terry," Joy's voice was only a whisper of desperate fear but Terry heard it.

His eyes darted toward her. Without another word but with his defiant head held high, Terald Benjamin Windthorn marched from the room.

For a long moment violent currents seemed to remain in the room, surging and crackling. With a groan, Skye put a trembling arm on the marble mantel and rested his head against it.

Joy sat silently in her chair. She felt flayed and beaten by the violence of the scene she had just witnessed. Her stomach was tied in multiple knots, and the palms of her hands were slippery and wet on the smooth leather of the chair arm.

"Okay! Say I told you so!" Skye's voice in the silent room made her start. "Tell me that I didn't accomplish anything by questioning Terry except make matters worse between us!"

Joy looked at him mutely.

"Well, at least I found out what I've suspected all along — Terry hates me!" he said bitterly.

Joy made a small protesting sound but Skye rushed on. Joy could sense anger building again in his voice. "And I found out for sure that he can talk if he wants to, and that he's been lying to me for three years while everyone ran circles about him trying to help the poor child!"

Skye's laugh was bitter and sarcastic. "Oh yes, he had everyone dancing a merry jig for him while I paid the fiddlers! I sold off my land and can't even keep this house properly repaired and heated because of the monstrous doctor bills!"

"I'm sure Terry never meant to be a burden, Mr. Windthorn. He is only a child and. . . ."

Skye turned on her savagely. "A very clever and vengeful child!"

"I don't believe he meant to hurt you when he pretended he couldn't talk. I still think he was afraid of revealing . . ."

". . . that horrible deed he is supposed to have done!" Skye finished maliciously. "I noticed that he never got around to telling us what it was!"

"You never let him finish his story!" Joy was losing her patience now, but she strove to keep her voice calm.

"I don't want you to see the boy anymore." Skye's voice was heavy with venom.

Thunderstruck, Joy asked, "But why?"

"Until he apologizes to me he won't be allowed to see you."

Joy stared at Skye for a moment before she said softly but clearly, "You are a cruel, selfish, unfeeling man. You don't deserve a fine son like Terry. You goad him into that tantrum and then blame him for the results."

Skye stood as if fastened to the floor, simply staring frozenly at her.

"Skye Windthorn, God will hold you accountable for what you make of that boy, whether he's your blood or not. I shudder to think what will happen to this house of hate if you don't learn the meaning of love. God stands ready to help, but He can't do a thing until you make him Lord of your life and ask His help."

Joy turned and went out the door leaving an angry fire burning in Skye Windthorn's eyes.

24

When Joy returned to her room, she saw that the waterfall picture was back in place and Kim was gone. Carole called to her and she went through the tiny adjoining hall to find Carole gingerly limping about the room without a crutch.

"I can put a little pressure on my left leg now," she said. "It will surely be good to be able to throw away the crutches." She sank down in a chair and raised her leg to a footstool.

As she did, she asked Joy, "Who do you think took Skye's scroll?"

Joy slowly shook her head, "I just don't know. But this could very well wreck Skye's career, I imagine, if it isn't found."

"I suppose Skye thinks his son stole it."

"Right. But Terry denies taking it. And I believe him — or maybe I should say, I want to believe him. Things are worse than ever between Terry and Skye now." Joy related the scene that had just transpired between the two. "Skye said I can't see Terry, but I plan to do so if it's humanly possible before we leave this place."

Joy tried unsuccessfully twice that afternoon to speak with Skye but Washington said he was busy. She considered seeing Terry against Skye's wishes but decided that would not be wise. Forced to remain in her room and do nothing, she hoped Terry would come to see her that night. But he did not come.

When she asked Washington that evening how Terry was, a mask seemed to slide down over his face and he gave a very vague, "He's all right, miss," before hurrying away.

The weatherman's forecast was the only encouraging news of the day. The storm was expected to end by morning.

When Kim brought in their meal that evening, Carole asked if the scroll had been found.

"No, ma'am, it hasn't. But Mr. Windthorn has notified the sheriff's department that it is missing," he said.

"He has? That must mean the phones are working again!" Carole exclaimed. "I can call David!"

"Has Mr. Windthorn decided Terry

didn't take it?" Joy asked, struggling with mixed relief and fear.

"That I wouldn't know, ma'am," Kim said respectfully. He plainly did not wish to discuss either the missing scroll or Terry.

Disheartened, Joy and Carole played a game of chess, but neither could keep her mind on the game. They played one game, then agreed to an early night, each hoping that this time the weather forecast had been right. Neither wanted to stay any longer now. Not even Carole's phone call to David could cheer them.

As soon as she awoke the next morning, Joy jumped from her bed and ran to the window. Rubbing off the frost, she peered out. Her heart gave a leap of joy. The snow had stopped and although clouds still hung over the trees, the wind had died down.

Joy raced into Carole's room with the happy news, but Carole was already up and dressed. When she burst in, Carole threw her arms around Joy in jubilation. "The storm's over and we're going back to the lodge. It seems like a month since I've seen David!"

There was a knock at the door. Kim stood there beaming his white-toothed grin. "Ladies, there are two gentlemen downstairs asking for you."

"Tell them we'll be right down," Carole said excitedly. "And thanks, Kim."

Carole and Joy quickly changed from their borrowed apparel into their own clothes and rushed downstairs as fast as Carole could limp on one crutch. There in the entryway David and Jeffrey, bundled in warm coats, stood talking with Kim and Washington. As soon as David saw Carole, he grabbed her and swung her from the stairs in a gleeful bearhug.

Joy felt warm and wanted again when Jeffrey's hazel brown eyes expressed his pleasure at the sight of her. "Are you all right?" Jeffrey's voice was anxious as he gave her a quick embrace.

"We're fine. Mr. Windthorn has been very kind to us," Joy assured him.

Carole disengaged herself from David's arms. "Washington, thank you so much for being such a good doctor!"

"My pleasure, ma'am," Washington's dark face crinkled into a smile.

Carole turned to Kim. "And thank you, too, for helping to make our stay so pleasant."

Kim only smiled shyly in answer.

"I also want to thank you both," Joy said. "You two have been great to us."

David spoke up. "Washington, would

you please tell Mr. Windthorn that we are deeply indebted to him. If there is ever anything that we can do for him, he has only to call."

Skye's slightly mocking voice answered them from the hall doorway. "I am sure we will not need your help, but you are gracious to offer." The faint smile on his face did not reach his eyes.

He advanced into the entryway. "I'm sorry to delay your departure but now that travel is once again possible, I must ask you to wait here until the sheriff arrives. He's just informed me that he is on his way. He wishes to question you ladies and the rest of us as well — about the missing scroll."

He moved toward Joy, held out a folded piece of paper to her, and said politely, "Here is the check I promised for working with Terry. Please accept it with my thanks for the effort you put forth to help him."

Joy protested but Skye pushed the check toward her. "I always pay my debts and will be offended if you refuse payment."

Joy put her hands in her pockets and spoke firmly, "And *I* will be offended if you force payment upon me. You took us in out of the storm and have done everything possible to make us comfortable.

Anything I did for Terry was a pleasure and bore its own reward."

Skye's unfathomable eyes held hers for a long moment before he said slowly, "Very well, we will consider it an even trade."

"Could I say goodbye to Terry?" Joy asked hesitantly. "I. . . ."

"I'm sorry, that won't be possible," Skye interrupted. "Terry has not complied with my wishes."

"I-if there is any way I can be a help — to Terry — let me know," Joy said quickly.

"Thank you, but I'm sure he will not need you again," Skye said curtly.

For some obscure reason, Joy felt her face grow hot and she turned away quickly to find Jeffrey watching her with a puzzled expression on his face. She gave him a weak smile.

"What's this about a missing scroll and the sheriff wanting to question the girls?" David asked Skye, breaking the tension that had descended. A sudden knock at the front door prevented Skye's answer.

Skye quickly opened the door to admit a paunchy middle-aged man with a star on his jacket, a burly deputy, and a rather dumpy, serious-faced woman. Skye introduced the men as Sheriff Scott and Deputy Morrow, and the woman as Eva, the sheriff's wife.

"I'm here about the valuable leather scroll that's missing," Sheriff Scott said as soon as the introductions were over. "It's my opinion that that thievin' cat burglar someway got through the blizzard and took it, but I'll need to hear everything anyone here knows about the scroll. I'm also goin' to have to search everyone."

"Is that really necessary, Sheriff?" Jeffrey expostulated. "I can vouch for these ladies. They're. . . ."

But the sheriff interrupted, "I'm just doin' my job, so let's get on with it. The missus will search the ladies."

Even David and Jeffrey had to submit to the search. "After all, one of the ladies could have slipped the scroll to one of you men," the sheriff declared.

Carole and Joy were escorted back upstairs for the search and questioned thoroughly. The rooms they had occupied were minutely examined.

Washington and Kim were interrogated and their rooms searched as well. But the scroll was not found.

Sheriff Scott apologized again for his actions but reiterated that he was just doing his job. "After all," he said, "I have to presume everyone is guilty 'til I discover who the real thief is. You are all free to go now and thanks for your cooperation."

"That makes you feel like a criminal, doesn't it?" Joy exclaimed as she and Carole followed David and Jeffrey outside.

As they climbed aboard the snowmobiles behind David and Jeffrey, Joy turned back for one last look at Windthorn. Its dark grey walls looked almost black in the gloom of the overcast sky. Skye and Prince stood motionless on the top step watching them. She shuddered. *If I never see this barren place again, it will please me well,* she thought. Then her heart gave a lurch. *But what of defenseless little Terry?* She felt like crying as the snowmobiles roared to life and headed back to the lodge.

Returning to the resort should have been a happy experience for Joy but, in spite of the enjoyable company of David, Carole — and Jeffrey — plus a call from her father and Mitzi, she couldn't seem to shake her apprehensions for Terry. And hovering somewhere around the edge of her heart was the insistent thought of his lonely, embittered father.

She even dreamed about them the first night back at the lodge — a crazy mixed-up nightmare. Terry was fleeing from her down a long, chilly hall at Windthorn,

238

looking back at her over his shoulder with wide, terrified eyes. In the shadows at the end of the hall, hidden from Terry, stood Skye, a mocking smile on his face. He reminded her of a vulture awaiting his unsuspecting victim. Joy was desperately afraid for Terry and ran after him calling his name but he wouldn't stop. She woke herself up, sobbing and calling his name.

The next morning, she told David and Carole about the dream. "I'm extremely concerned about Terry," Joy finished. "I can't seem to get him off my mind even at night.

"He despises his father and I can hardly blame him. I honestly feel that Skye means well by Terry, and probably even loves him, but he doesn't know the first thing about how to deal with Terry. I don't know what will become of him if he remains with his father."

"You don't suppose Skye would let someone else take Terry to raise?" David asked.

"I'm sure he wouldn't," Joy said. "He is a strange man but he has a strong feeling of responsibility for the boy. Skye would feel he was neglecting that responsibility if he let someone else take him, but that might be the only thing that would heal the hurt in Terry."

"It isn't going to be easy, no matter what happens," Carole said thoughtfully. "But both of us had difficult childhoods and God still reached into our lives. He can do the same for Terry. Let's pray and ask God to work it out His way."

25

Carole gave the golden curls shimmering on Joy's finely shaped head a final pat. "There! You look like a fairy princess. You'll have Jeffrey tongue-tied with admiration."

Joy laughed with pleasure. Standing up, she turned slowly in front of the large mirror, examining every line of the long, beautifully cut, deep rose evening gown. Satisfied with what she saw, she said gratefully, "Thanks to your help with my hair, I do look okay, don't I?"

"That's the understatement of the year," Carole scoffed. "You're gorgeous!" She sobered. "This must be a very important date with Jeffrey. Dinner in his own private dining room — and formal, at that. I peeked in there a while ago and the room is lovely with fresh flowers and candles. The table is just beautiful. Jeffrey has really gone all out for you."

Joy laughed softly. "Jeffrey is so sweet

and thoughtful. His wife will be a lucky girl."

"Is there any doubt who that will be?" Carole said. She was smiling, but there was a very real question in the seriousness of her dark eyes.

A troubled, slightly distressed expression suddenly came into Joy's face, and she hesitated before she spoke. "I want to love Jeffrey," she said, "but I still don't know if I do. He is everything a girl could want in a husband but. . . ."

"He doesn't set your heart to racing like crazy."

"Right! I respect him enormously. I'm very fond of him, and he is great fun to be with, but I just don't know if I love him."

"Three weeks is a very short time for real love to develop," Carole said. "And I still say that God will direct you. Even though I think Jeffrey Pitman is the catch of the year and you two look great together, don't let yourself be rushed into anything before *you* are sure." Carole impulsively hugged Joy. "That's my big sisterly advice, for what it's worth."

"Thanks," Joy said appreciatively. She glanced at her watch. "Jeffrey will be here any minute. Carole, I really appreciate your help — and the advice." She dabbed perfume on her wrists and earlobes and reached for a small evening purse.

Fifteen minutes later, Joy sat opposite Jeffrey in his cozy, private dining room. She felt a little lightheaded with the knowledge of the expense and attention that had been given to making the room enchanting and beautiful for their first date alone. They had ice skated together, gone on various resort activities as a couple and dined together with others, but they had never been alone until now.

Soft music, glowing candles, the fragrance and beauty of expensive hothouse flowers, shining silver, and lovely, delicate china all united to create a magical, romantic atmosphere.

Joy enjoyed the meal and Jeffrey's company enormously. He was highly complimentary about her appearance, making her feel very special.

Over dessert and coffee, they listened to a new record album that was one of his favorites. When it had finished, Jeffrey rose to put on a Praise Strings album, then came to sit beside her on the sofa. Taking one of her hands in his, he looked deeply into her eyes, saying nothing for a long moment. Finally breaking the silence, he said quietly, "Joy, I think I'm falling in love with you."

Unexpectedly, a flood of dismay rather than happiness set her heart to pounding painfully and showed in her expressive face as he rushed on. "I know this is too soon to be talking to you about love. But I want you to know that you are the most wonderful woman I have ever met. I want so much to be able to spend more time with you, getting to know you and opening the doors of our hearts to each other."

"Jeffrey," Joy said softly, "you are so sweet. You are the kindest, most thoughtful and generous man I've ever met. But you're right. It is too early to speak of love. Can we just be good friends for now?"

Jeffrey grinned, undaunted by her question, "As long as I'm your special friend. But if I have my way, we'll become much more than good friends!"

26

It was evening of the next day and the sun had shone brilliantly all day. Now, it was going down behind a snow-shrouded mountain, bathing the world in glorious golden light.

Skye lay on a long leather lounge in his study with a reference book in hand. Suddenly, with a muttered exclamation, he threw the large volume on the floor with so much force that Washington stuck his head in the door.

"Is anything wrong, Mr. Windthorn?"

"No-no. A book just fell on the floor," Skye answered irritably, sitting up.

Washington moved into the room. "Is there any news about the missing scroll?"

"Sheriff Scott hasn't turned up anything so far," Skye said. "How's Terry?"

Washington grimaced. "He still hasn't touched a bite." Anxiety etched deep lines in his dark face. "I'm worried, Mr. Windthorn. That boy can't afford to go without nourishment like this. He's not got enough flesh on his bones as it is."

"Don't you think I know that!" snapped Skye.

"What do you suggest, sir? I'm baffled. Those wailing spells take a lot out of the child and he's had two since the ladies left. I hate to give him those powerful tranquilizers so often."

"I know — I know!" Skye said testily. "We may have to put him back in the hospital. He's got to eat even if we have to feed him intravenously."

"Perhaps if you tried to talk to him, gentle-like," Washington suggested hesitantly.

"I've tried to talk to him every way I know how," Skye said wearily, "and I get nowhere. He just stares at me without saying a word." He closed his eyes and rubbed a slightly unsteady hand over them. "Maybe I don't know how to talk — gentle," he admitted, "but I swear to you, I've tried."

Washington sighed. "I haven't been able to get him to talk to me either. He just seems to have retreated from the whole world."

Skye looked at Washington helplessly,

246

his bloodshot eyes and grey, haggard face revealing his strain, worry and sleepless nights. "I think he blames me for Mrs. Kyle leaving. The only words he has spoken to me were, 'Where is Joy?' When I said she had gone back to the resort, he gave me a murderous look and turned his back on me. I've threatened and I've reasoned but he hasn't said a word since."

"Maybe we could get the lady to come back for . . ."

"No! She wouldn't come anyway!"

"Begging your pardon, sir, but I believe she would. She's one nice lady! She seemed to really take to the boy and she knew just how to handle him." Washington was talking fast. "I could run over to the resort on a snowmobile to get her."

"It's out of the question!" Skye said sharply.

"But, sir. . . ."

"I said no! And that settles it!"

"Yes, sir," Washington said shortly as he left the room with a solemn face.

Skye sank back on the lounge wearily and closed his eyes. Unbidden, a picture of Joy Kyle rose into his mind: soft, blond hair; blue eyes like a vivid, rainwashed summer sky; full, exquisitely formed lips curved into a gentle smile.

Skye sat up abruptly and shook his head savagely. He ran long, slender fingers into his dark, crisp hair, clenched them and yanked. The pain cleared his mind of her image.

He sat there on the side of the lounge with his head in his hands. "It isn't enough that Terry is about to drive me out of my mind," he said aloud, "but that — that girl won't let me alone, either."

Something akin to a sob rose in his throat. What was wrong with him? For four days now — almost from the moment she had walked out his door, Joy Kyle had been with him. Sometimes it was her image, sometimes her voice. Every word she had spoken to him while in this house seemed to be stored in his mind. And, with no effort on his part, his mind would play it back to him, word for word.

Or her picture would float into his mind, so intensely real he could smell the perfume she wore and see the sparkle in her eyes. Sometimes she was smiling, sometimes she was serious, and twice she was crying. His meticulous mind had registered every tilt of her head, the gracefulness of her walk, the loveliness of her face. Now bits and pieces rolled through his mind, leaving him an unwilling but powerless spectator.

The hurt of Lillian's betrayal was still a deep, unhealed wound inside him and he had vowed never to become involved with another woman after his wife's tragic death. And it hadn't been hard; because of his work he seldom associated with women and when he did, his barbed tongue sent them skittering away. In spite of her coquetry, Skye had loved Lillian deeply. He never had known quite how to articulate that love, but it had nonetheless been very real and very intense.

So this continuous bombardment of Joy Kyle into his mind was a puzzle to Skye. He had admittedly been impressed with her sweet face and her gentle, caring spirit. But Lillian had seemed to possess those virtues, too — until he was married to her. Pain, almost like a knife blow, struck deep into his heart as he recalled his marriage. He had thought Lillian so perfect, so lovely, so sweet, so loving.

Joy's soft voice obtruded into his reveries, causing him to start. Though not audible, the words came just as forcefully as though they were. *I shudder to think what will happen to this house of hate if you don't learn the meaning of love.*

"You're blaming *me* for everything!" he exclaimed aloud and then felt foolish. He was answering a voice in his mind.

He strove to think of something else, anything else, but Joy's face surfaced again in his memory, accusing but sad. He groaned aloud.

Was he, Skye Windthorn, really to blame for the tangled mess his life had become? Doubts and suspicions that he was at least partly to blame had tried to creep into his mind at different times in the past three years, but he had always rejected them. After all, he was not the unfaithful one, the traitor to their marriage!

But suddenly he could not seem to expel the thoughts of his own guilt. *Perhaps I'm just too tired and discouraged to fight them anymore,* he thought. And the questions flooded into his mind. Had he made this a house of hate even before Lillian died? Had he failed Lillian in some way? He had loved her with his whole heart, but as soon as he realized her desire for the attentions of other men, he had begun to criticize, censure and revile her.

She had been a spoiled only child from a home that idolized her. Could it be that he had only seen *his* needs and had not met her need to feel secure in his love? He had felt her flirtations as a threat to his ego and had not tried to find out the cause of them.

Perhaps there was nothing he could have done; Lillian might have just been a hopeless coquette. But he had never tried to talk with her about it; he had only railed and disparaged her in their ever escalating fights.

Unable to halt the march of them, his thoughts were as shocking and as corrosive as acid in his mind. Helpless before their brutal onslaught, Terry's words suddenly forced their way into his mind. *Mamma loved me, but you never did! You said I wasn't even your son! Well, I don't want to be your son! I hate you!*

"Oh, God, am I guilty of making my son hate me, too?" He scarcely realized that the cry was a real prayer, to a God his skeptical mind had refused to believe existed. "No! I refuse to believe that I'm the only one guilty for the hate in this house. Lillian turned that child against me! I know she did!"

But the inexorable voice of Joy Kyle insinuated itself into his conscience. *Perhaps she didn't turn Terry against you.*

"Maybe it wasn't Lillian," Skye groaned aloud. "Maybe *I* turned Terry against me. I left the care of him first to Lillian and then to Washington. We hardly know each other. If Terry equates love with the time

I've spent with him, he could easily conclude I didn't love him."

Well, do I really love him? The question demanded an answer. *I think so,* Skye conceded hesitantly. *Otherwise, why have I spent so much money on his health? To fulfill my obligation? To appease the feelings of guilt that keep trying to wrap their slimy tentacles around me?*

The idea had festered in him for a long time that Terry might be the child of a lover of Lillian's and not his own son. Now, he admitted to himself, that possibility had chilled his feelings for the boy at times. Also, Terry's strong resemblance to his unfaithful mother had not been in his favor, either, he reluctantly acknowledged.

I'm trying to be honest, he thought. *Perhaps for the first time since Lillian died, but I'm not even sure of my own feelings. And I'm too tired to battle any of this anymore right now. I do hope Terry sleeps tonight. If he has another of those wailing episodes, I think I'll go bury myself in a snowbank!*

But neither Washington's nor Skye's rest was disturbed that night. And, totally exhausted, both slept later than usual.

It was Kim who brought the bad news to Skye's bedroom the next morning, awakening him with a loud knock on the door.

Irritated at being aroused from his first deep sleep in days, Skye called grumpily, "What do you want?"

Kim's dark eyes were wide with alarm as he stepped into the room. "Mr. Windthorn, s-sir, the boy isn't in his room and. . . ."

"What do you mean Terry isn't in his room?" Skye was fully awake now. "Maybe he went down to his mother's room."

"No, sir, he isn't there either! I've looked everywhere for him. I-I didn't want to wake you or Washington, but I'm frightened, sir!"

Thirty minutes later, Washington, Skye, and Kim had thoroughly searched the house. Terry was, indeed, missing. And Prince — plus his leash — was also gone!

Skye usually left his door ajar at night and if Prince wanted to go outdoors, he let himself out through a dog-door in the kitchen. Impeccably obedient, he always came immediately at a call from his master. But no amount of calling produced the dog this morning.

Washington searched Terry's room and found other items missing . . . items that had belonged to Skye when he was a boy: a pair of snowshoes, a heavy sweater, ski pants, a sheepskin coat, two pairs of wool socks, a fur lined cap and a ski mask.

Pointing to a book on survival in snow country lying on the desk, Washington said heavily, "Not two months ago, Terry seemed interested in survival skills and to humor him, I bought that book. I even dug out those old snowshoes and that old snow gear of yours from when you were about his age."

His dark eyes were stark with fear and his voice shook, "Sir, I never thought he would ever try to use them, or I-I. . . ."

Skye laid an unsteady hand on Washington's arm. "Don't blame yourself, it's been hard to outthink that kid. I imagine he's trying to go to Joy — Mrs. Kyle, don't you?"

"That would be my guess," Washington said. "At least he didn't go without some preparation. If we get right on his trail, he shouldn't be harmed."

"Right!" Skye said, but he wasn't as optimistic as he tried to sound. He knew that Terry, small for his age and unskilled in the actual use of snowshoes on deep snow, faced enormous odds. And how could he know the direction to take?

"That Terry is a smart boy," Kim said a little too heartily, "and remember, sir, he has Prince."

Skye agreed aloud, but in his mind, he was seeing a fragile, little eight-year-old, struggling over a wide expanse of snow and a treacherous, unforgiving landscape.

The cry that rose into his mind was a real prayer, *Merciful God, please help us find him. Don't let him die out there!* He turned quickly from the others so they couldn't see the sudden rush of tears that blinded his eyes.

27

It was almost noon when Skye and Kim parked their two snowmobiles on the snow heaped lawn of Forest Lakes Lodge and sprinted to the wide entrance. They nearly collided with Jeffrey Pitman who was coming out.

Jeffrey's cordial greeting died on his lips when he saw Skye's face. "What's wrong?" he exclaimed.

"The boy," Skye said, "my son — is he here?"

"Not that I know of," Jeffrey said in bewilderment. "Should he be?"

"Terry has apparently run away," Skye said through taut lips, "and we are sure he was trying to come to Mrs. Kyle. Is she here?"

"In the dining room. I'll show you," Jeffrey said, quickly leading the way.

They crossed the lobby with long, impatient strides, passed down a wide hall and turned to the left through double doors. "This way," Jeffrey said. He threaded his way around oak tables spread with snowy linen cloths and filled with well-dressed vacationers who sat laughing and talking.

Joy was the first to spy Jeffrey, with Skye and Kim close behind him, coming toward their table. Her face paled when she saw Skye's set face.

She half-raised from her chair. "Has something happened to Terry?" she asked in alarm.

"Terry has run away." Ignoring the others, Skye moved to face her. "We were sure he tried to find you. Have you seen him?"

"N-no, I haven't! When did he leave Windthorn?"

"He was gone when I checked on him at eight this morning," Kim answered.

"Are you sure he isn't hiding somewhere in the house?" Joy questioned, refusing to admit the fear demanding entry into her heart and mind.

"We thought of that," Skye said bleakly. "We have searched every inch of the house and even the outbuildings."

David spoke from across the table, "We'll get a search party together and help you hunt for him!"

"Thank you . . ." Skye began earnestly, but Jeffrey interrupted.

"I'll go to my office and use the loud-speaker to find out how many resort guests we can get to help. We'll alert Dr. Hestley to stand by. The lodge's helicopter is always ready and we can use it to search the area by air."

"Good," Skye said, "I was wishing I hadn't sold mine. Of course I'll pay all the expenses incurred."

Jeffrey waved the suggestion aside with an impatient hand. "I'll put in a call to the Forest Rangers' station, too," Jeffrey added. "A ranger may want to talk to you, Skye, for a description and anything else that might help."

David started to rise but Jeffrey said quickly, "David, why don't you finish your lunch? You're liable to need it. I've had mine. Skye, let's go to my office." He moved swiftly to the outer edge of the room and toward the doorway. Skye and Kim followed.

At the door, Jeffrey stopped a waitress. "Bring some hot coffee and sandwiches to my office for these men right away."

As the three men passed out into the hall, Skye felt a gentle tug at his arm. Looking down, he saw that Joy had followed them.

258

A sudden inexplicable quiver shot through Skye as he looked into Joy's face. Her soft voice was tremulous; her eyes warm with concern. "How has Terry been — these past four days?"

"Not good," Skye said honestly, no longer able to deny the truth. He felt a warm glow of appreciation for Joy's concern as she fell into step beside him. "We haven't been fighting anymore," he said ruefully, "but Terry hasn't been eating or talking. We were considering putting him in the hospital." He made a hopeless gesture, "And now this!"

"We'll find him!" Joy said confidently, laying her hand on his arm. "God will help us."

"We've *got* to find him before dark," Skye said. "If we don't . . ." His voice trailed off.

"I want to help," Joy said. "I noticed Washington wasn't with you so I presume he stayed at Windthorn in case Terry returns." At Skye's nod, Joy continued, "Could I take his place there so he would be free to help search, too?"

Gratitude shone in Skye's eyes and was reflected in his voice. "That is very kind of you, especially when I treated you so rudely when. . . ."

"It doesn't matter," Joy said.

"I'll be flying the helicopter," Jeffrey broke in, having heard their conversation. "I can drop you off and pick up Washington."

They were at the door of Jeffrey's office now. "Do you have any two-way radios?" Jeffrey asked Skye.

"Three," Skye replied. "Washington will know where they are."

"Good. There are several here and the ranger station will have some, too," Jeffrey said.

"We'll leave one with Joy at Windthorn," Skye said. He turned to Joy, "Washington is making up a big kettle of stew in case we had to form a search party. The men will need food and lots of hot coffee. You could take over that department, if you don't mind."

"Be glad to," she agreed. She hesitated outside the door to Jeffrey's office and then asked, "Have you found the scroll, yet?"

Skye paused, too, meeting her clear blue eyes with his pain-filled ones. "No, but it seems rather unimportant now."

As the guests heard about the problem, several of the expert skiers volunteered their help. Jeffrey reported that the ranger station had contacted a local Job Corps camp, which was about an hour's drive away, and that a truckload of young men would be arriving as soon as possible. The rangers would be helping as well as coordinating the search.

"With all this help, we should soon have that boy safely back home," Jeffrey told Skye confidently.

But by the end of the day things did not look hopeful. The light snow that had fallen the night before had wiped out all traces of Terry's snowshoes. And the weather forecast predicted more snow that night.

Searchers on snowmobiles, on skis, and on snowshoes had crisscrossed the area between Windthorn and the resort but found absolutely no sign of the boy or dog. Jeffrey, with the doctor as a passenger, had flown back and forth over the area with no results at all.

"If Prince is within hearing distance of our voices, he would bark," Skye told Jeffrey over the radio, puzzled. "Unless, of course, they are. . . ." he left the terrible possibility unsaid.

At nightfall, most of the searchers, including the rangers, gave up the search until morning. "We don't want to lose a man over a cliff," the head ranger explained to Skye. "But we'll be out again in the morning as soon as it's light enough to see."

David, Skye, Kim and Washington continued to look until almost nine o'clock.

"Skye," David placed a hand on Skye's shoulder before he turned his snowmobile homeward, "if you fall into a canyon, you can't search tomorrow. We're all nearly dead with fatigue. It's best if you give it up tonight."

"Before long," Skye said wearily. "I'll see you in the morning. And thanks so much!"

"You go on home, too," Skye told Washington.

"You shouldn't stay out here alone. You had better follow David's advice," Washington remonstrated.

"I will, soon," Skye said.

They had arrived back at the road which led to Windthorn from the main highway. During the day, a bulldozer had cleared it, and the snow was piled in high banks on either side. With a last look at Skye, Washington and David unwillingly glided away on their snowmobiles.

Skye stood alone by his snowmobile, uncorked a thermos, and drank the last of the remaining lukewarm coffee. He looked up at the sky. A few stars glittered weakly and a pale yellow moon struggled to emerge from behind a grey cloud. Skye shivered, but not from the cold. His mind was visualizing a frail little boy somewhere out in that harsh, forbidding expanse of forest and snow — cold, terrified and utterly helpless.

His eyes misted and then he felt hot tears running down his face. Was it only last night that he had wondered if he really loved Terry? Now his heart throbbed with pain and anguish. Did he love that boy who might not even be his natural son? Yes! There was no doubt in his mind now. If Terry died, he wasn't sure he could go on living — wasn't sure he would want to. That skinny little boy was as much a part of him as a hand or leg.

A sob rose in his throat. He sank down on the snowmobile seat and put his head in his arms on the steering wheel. Shuddering sobs shook his lean frame for several moments.

Then softly, like the velvet brush of butterfly wings, Joy's words echoed in his mind. *God stands ready to help but He can't do a thing until you believe in His Son, make Christ Lord of your life, and ask His help.*

"I do!" Skye cried aloud into the cold and dark night. "I accept you, Jesus, as the

Lord of my life, if you will only help me find my boy!"

You are a cruel, selfish, unfeeling man. You don't deserve a son like Terry. Joy's unrelenting words spoke again somewhere inside him.

"I know! I know! Dear God, forgive me! Please forgive me." For a long while Skye sobbed out his shame, his fears for Terry, and pled for God's help. After a while his cries sank to a whisper. Then Skye straightened up and wiped his face with a large wrinkled handkerchief he found in the pocket of his fur lined coat.

He felt drained and exhausted — and uncertain. Had God really heard his prayers and accepted them? He didn't feel any different. But Joy had said confidently that God stood ready to help, if he would only give his life to God, hadn't she? Could he just accept that God would do His part now?

A chilling thought struck him. Would he still serve God if Terry were dead? That the child was already dead was a horrible possibility that he had to face. His mind shrieked, *No! He can't be dead!* But he had to think about this rationally. Could he — would he — still live for God if Terry was gone?

A vivid picture of the bleakness of his life to this point rose in his mind. It was a life that had been lived only to please Skye Windthorn. He winced. Joy, David, Carole, and even Jeffrey, were all what he had sneeringly called fanatical Christians, but he had never known such caring, loving people. And he couldn't remember when he had been as joyful and peaceful as they were.

He, Skye Windthorn, had always lived for himself, regardless of whom he had hurt — even Lillian whom he had loved so dearly; Terry — and Washington, who was more a loyal, trusted friend than an employee. The list rolled through his mind in self-condemning judgment. And he had failed them all because Skye Windthorn had bowed at one shrine and one only — the shrine of self-gratification!

Skye writhed in shame under the cold, brutal light of his own soul examination. He felt stripped and naked and utterly bereft. "I need you, God," he whispered hoarsely, "not just your help to find my son but to change this wretched creature that I am! I believe in your Son. Forgive me."

Slow tears again ran off his face but they were tears of total surrender. And at last, as Skye lifted his wet face to the dark sky, a peace like he had never known began to filter into his barren spirit until it became a warm, healing stream that seemed to surge through every fragment of his body and soul.

Skye Windthorn felt like he had come home!

28

When David radioed Joy that they were returning to the resort, Jeffrey picked Joy up at Windthorn in his helicopter.

On the flight back to the lodge, Jeffrey filled Joy in on the disheartening news of the day's fruitless search. "That poor little kid," Jeffrey said, "the temperature's going to be below zero tonight. He doesn't have much chance of surviving."

"I wish Terry had never seen me," Joy said passionately, with tears in her eyes, "then maybe he wouldn't have run away!"

Jeffrey reached over and laid his free hand on Joy's hands, knotted together on her lap. "You can't blame yourself. If anyone is to blame, it is Skye. I feel sorry for him, but he hasn't been much of a father to the child. He's gone a lot of the time and from what I've been able to tell, he ignores him when he's home."

"He does love Terry, though," Joy said quickly.

"Most of the time he's a pretty unpleasant man," Jeffrey said. "If Skye's that way with Terry, I understand why he thinks his father hates him."

"You've only seen Skye in adverse situations," Joy answered defensively. "I had dinner with him a couple of times while we were at Windthorn, and he was charming company, a perfect host. He can be very warm and kind."

Jeffrey was silent for a moment as he began to bring the helicopter down. Then he said quizzically, "Skye Windthorn hasn't been working his way into your affections, has he?"

Joy felt the hot blood rush into her face and she answered too quickly, "Skye is a dedicated woman-hater. And if he weren't, I've had my fill of tyrants. My father was one before he came to Christ, and so was my late husband."

Jeffrey set the helicopter down neatly on its pad and then turned to Joy. "Let's forget about Skye and go have some supper. Just the two of us. What do you say?"

"If you like," Joy said. She looked away toward the dark line of forest and mountains and said slowly, "but I'm not sure I can do it justice tonight. I keep thinking of little Terry out there somewhere." She looked up at Jeffrey through misty blue eyes. "Jeffrey, he is a dear little thing." Her voice broke and she turned her head away.

Jeffrey's warm, hazel brown eyes lingered on Joy. "That was really kind of you to put yourself out today for Skye when he was so rude to you the other day. You're quite a girl!"

Joy protested but Jeffrey laid a finger on her lips. "I've never met anyone like you before." His voice had gone husky with emotion and he finished softly, "You are not only lovely, but you are caring and thoughtful and everything I ever dreamed of finding in a woman. I had begun to wonder if there was anyone like you left in the world."

Joy felt color tinging her cheeks again. "Please don't say such things; you're embarrassing me."

"I would like to say a lot more, but I guess dinner might be a more romantic place to say them."

Joy became very still for a moment, then she said gently, "Jeffrey, I like you very much and I enjoy your company. And at this point, that's all I want in a relationship. Can you understand what I mean?" Her voice was almost a plea.

Jeffrey put up a placating hand. "I guess that will have to do for now. I promise to not tell you again of how beautiful you are and how I would go to the ends of the earth to make you happy and. . . ." His eyes were twinkling and his voice teasing.

Joy laughed. "And you're impossible! Let's go eat before you get any worse."

29

Long before the sun rose over the mountain rim, Skye and a large search party were once more combing the forested slopes. Today, at Skye's suggestion, the men had divided into four parties, each taking a different direction on the possibility that Terry might have become confused and even gone in the opposite direction from the resort. He had gotten only vague directions from Washington the day Carole and Joy left — to Washington's dismay now.

Skye had decided to use cross-country skis today instead of the snowmobile so he could hear sounds better. If Terry had fallen into a crevasse or was hurt, his voice might be faint. A call could be heard much farther if there were no motor noise to mask it.

Skye left his estate by the newly-plowed road that wound its way to the highway, following it for a short while before he struck off into the deep, unbroken snow in the opposite direction from the resort. He was an experienced and toughened cross-country skier and though the terrain was rugged, he traveled easily and smoothly.

Skye moved slowly, calling loudly every minute or two until his voice was hoarse and his throat raspy. His keen eyes were ever roving, scanning every rill and mound, examining any odd color against the white snow; his ears alert for any strange sound.

By noon his eyes were burning and his throat was sore but he pushed on after a quick drink of hot coffee from his light backpack. Sticking a piece of elk jerky in his mouth, he chewed methodically as he skied.

He hadn't heard the sound of anyone else for a long while. *Perhaps I should turn back,* he thought. *Surely a child could not have come this far.* Consulting his compass, he turned at a right angle to the path he had come and traveled perhaps a quarter of a mile before turning back toward Windthorn.

Periodically all day, Skye had talked to God. Although still gravely concerned about Terry, he possessed a calmness today that had not been there yesterday. He had even slept some last night.

Now night was coming on again. Discouragement dogged his lagging steps. He tried not to think of Terry alone in this vast, merciless wilderness for another night. He stopped and rested a moment. His eyes swept the terrain, squinting through reddened lids. Noticing a small, swift rill wending its way through the snowy banks, he glided over to get a drink. He was exhausted, almost numb, and his throat felt parched.

Removing his skis and a mitten, he knelt at the ice encrusted edge of the small stream and dipped up some of the frigid water. His hand froze midway to his mouth. Lying under the lip of the ice, almost in the water, was a small, bedraggled brown stuffed dog!

"Sparky!" Skye's heart gave a mighty lurch. He sprang up and swept the glistening snow with wide, excited eyes, his weariness forgotten. But there were no breaks in the smooth, heaped snow. Skye slowly, almost reverently, pocketed Terry's ragged little toy dog.

For a long moment he stood silently, thinking. Terry must have drunk from this very stream! What would he have done then? Slowly a thought began to take shape. If Terry were aware at this point that he was lost, then he would probably have resorted to the survival knowledge he had gleaned from Washington and the survival manual. Reaching way back into his past, Skye could hear Washington instructing him at about age ten, "If you are ever lost, find a stream, if possible, and follow it down. Streams eventually go down to a house or town — and people."

Skye searched the immediate area thoroughly, calling as he went. Then, satisfied that Terry was not in this area, he returned quickly to the stream and turned downhill. As he followed the stream, he stopped often, calling Terry's and Prince's names and searching the snow for any sign that Terry — or Prince — had been there.

The grueling trek was telling on Skye by the time the sun had begun to sink below the mountain peaks. His steps were dragging and his breath came in ragged gasps. Dispirited and almost totally drained, Skye removed his skis and sank down on a fallen log.

"It's going to be dark soon," he said aloud. "Dear God — Father — you are a Father, too. You understand how I feel better than anyone else ever could. You had to watch your Son suffer. Please have mercy on me. Don't let Terry have to spend another night out in this cold! Please!" He had to quickly blank out of his mind the picture that had risen there of fragile little Terry — terrified, freezing and sobbing in the cold darkness.

Summoning the last reserves of his strength and knowing he needed energy to force his exhausted limbs into motion again, he pulled a chocolate candy bar from his pack and apathetically peeled back the wrapper.

The forest was very quiet, almost hushed. Before he took a bite, he lifted up his hoarse voice and shouted, "Terry! Prince!" He raised the candy bar to his mouth — and froze.

Had he heard something? The sound was so faint that for a moment, he couldn't believe he had. Then it came again. Was it a dog barking? The sound was so faint that he wasn't sure.

He shouted again with all the strength in him, then cupped his hands behind his ears. This time the sound was unmistakably distinguishable — a series of rapid barks. His heart began to hammer. "Easy, Skye," he cautioned aloud, "it could be a searcher's dog or. . . ."

Another sound joined the barking. A

human voice, very faint.

Stuffing the candy bar into his coat pocket, Skye yelled again and tried to judge the direction the barking was coming from when it came again. Moving slowly at first until he was certain of the direction, then more rapidly, Skye continued to call. As the sounds grew more pronounced and louder, he became more and more certain that the bark came from Prince.

The sun had dipped below the treetops by now and the light was swiftly disappearing. Skye could hear the barks clearly but still could not see the Great Dane. In the dusk, he moved forward cautiously.

Suddenly, almost at his feet, a child's voice called, "Be careful, there's a cliff!"

Skye felt waves of joy roll through him. The voice was hoarse — but unmistakably the voice of his son!

"Terry! Where are you?"

At the sound of Skye's voice so close, Prince went wild with joyful barking. Finally Skye had to command him to be quiet before he subsided to a desperate whimper.

"We're on a shelf down below you," Terry called through the gloom.

"Are you all right?"

There was a pause and Skye heard a

tremor in Terry's weak voice. "I-I think my leg is broken."

Skye felt a finger of fear race down his spine. It was night and they were a long way from help. Calming his fears with a quickly breathed prayer, Skye called, "I have a flashlight in my backpack. Don't move and I'll get it."

A few seconds later, Skye was lying on his stomach in the snow, focusing the beam over the cliff and down. The light stabbed into the darkness and Skye could see a small shelf of rock perhaps ten or twelve feet below. It looked precariously narrow from his perspective. The shelf was on the side of a deep crack in the mountainside. He still could not see Terry or Prince.

"Where are you? I can't see you."

"Be still, Prince," Skye heard, and he saw the back end of Prince for a second before it disappeared. "We're in a little cave under the ledge," Terry said. "Prince is getting so excited that I'm afraid he'll fall off. I'm holding him."

Confident of his dog's training, Skye commanded, "Lie down, Prince."

"He's lying down now," Terry reported. "C-can you get us out?" The hoarse voice had risen a little and Skye sensed that the child was striving to keep calm but was bordering on hysteria.

"Don't you worry about a thing," Skye said emphatically. "We'll get you out! Just sit tight while I call for some help on the two-way radio."

Skye quickly removed his radio. "This is Skye Windthorn. Does anyone read me?"

Skye listened anxiously. There was no answer.

He tried again. "This is Skye Windthorn, the father of the lost child. Does anyone hear me?"

The radio crackled and then a familiar voice spoke, "Mr. Windthorn, this is Washington. Have you found Terry?" Hope rang in his voice.

"That I have! Where are you?"

"I'm about a mile southwest of Windthorn. Is Terry all right?"

Another voice broke in. "Hey, Skye, this is Jeffrey. That's great news about Terry! I'm in the helicopter with Dr. Hestley. Is there a clearing nearby large enough to land in?"

"There's one not too far away," Skye said. "I'll give you my position and put out a flare here, then go down and see about Terry. When I figure out his situation, I'll climb back up, find that clearing and outline it in flares."

278

Skye consulted his compass and a forest service map and gave directions.

"We're on our way," Jeffrey said. "We'll circle until you get the flares set. Over and out."

"I'll be there soon, too, Mr. Windthorn," Washington's voice crackled out. "This old snowmobile has just received a new burst of energy."

"Help's on the way," Skye called down to Terry. "I'm going to tie a rope to this tree and come down to you." He kept talking to keep Terry's mind busy.

"Okay, the rope's knotted to the tree. Now, I'm going to find a little firewood and send it down." Forgetting his tiredness, Skye scrambled about in the snow, dragging out two dead branches that he could break up easily without a hatchet. "Are you cold?" he said, trying to keep Terry talking and as busy as possible.

"Y-yes."

"We'll take care of that right away. I'm tying the wood to the rope, now. Here it comes; don't let it knock you or Prince off the shelf." He slowly lowered the wood until Terry called that it was there.

Skye again detected a near-the-breaking-point quiver in the voice. He had to get down there as quickly as possible!

"I'm setting out a flare up here. Can you start breaking off some of the smaller pieces of wood and get them ready to start a fire with?" Skye said briskly.

Terry's voice had steadied again. "Okay."

A minute later Skye called, "I'm coming down."

Within seconds he was standing on the ledge — which was much wider than it had appeared from above — with Prince dancing around him in joyous welcome. Skye fondled and praised the dog, but his eyes were probing the murky depths of the small cave.

Snapping on his flashlight, Skye shone its beam into the opening. He saw in a glance that the cave was really only a deep recess under the rock. Terry was sitting with his back against the wall. His face looked small and pinched under the heavy fur lined cap. His mittened hands were breaking off small twigs and branches from the dead tree limb that he had drawn toward him.

Heavy fur lined boots — Skye recognized them as his from a long dim past — encased Terry's small feet. One of the boots was unlaced and the foot was propped between two rocks.

All of these things registered in Skye's first quick scan. Silencing Prince's wild barking with a sharp command, Skye stooped and crawled into the low shelter with the flashlight still in his hand.

The boy dropped the branch he was breaking apart and lifted his face to gaze at Skye. He seemed to straighten his shoulders and his face took on a stiffly defiant look that could only thinly veil the fear and dread clearly defined in Terry's wide blue eyes.

"I guess you're awful mad at me." His voice was low, more of a statement than a question.

Skye crawled toward Terry and squatted by his side before he answered. In fact, it was difficult to answer at all for a moment around the fist-sized lump that had formed in his throat. He laid the light down so that it illuminated their faces before he said gently, "No, Terry, I'm not angry."

Disbelief sprang into Terry's eyes as he stammered, "Y-you a-aren't? B-but I ran a-away and . . . and . . ."

"All that matters is that my son is safe," Skye said softly.

Terry lowered his head, then looked up at Skye through eyelashes that shone golden in the gleam of the flashlight. "But you said I might not be your son."

Skye's eyes misted and he said huskily,

"Whether I fathered you or not, you are my son!" His voice trembled, then cracked, "Son, if you only knew how much I love you! I've been worried almost out of my mind. You mean more than life to me!"

For a long moment, the blue eyes stared at Skye in doubt. Then the small face crumpled and Terry burst into tears.

Skye gathered him into his arms. For a moment the small, bundled form was stiff in his embrace. Then it went limp as Terry's arms went round Skye's neck in almost a death clutch and the boy sobbed brokenly on his father's shoulder.

For a long while Skye held the boy tightly in his arms, letting him cry. He felt a fierce, protective joy coursing through every fiber of his body. *Dear God,* he prayed silently, *while I have been preoccupied with pleasing Skye Windthorn, I have missed the pleasure of being a real father! Thank you for giving me a second chance. Thank you for Terry — my son.*

And at that moment, Skye Windthorn wouldn't have traded places with the richest man on earth!

30

When Terry's tears were spent, Skye asked gently, "Are you all right now, son?"

Terry drew away and nodded his head.

"Does your leg hurt badly?"

"Not too bad unless I move it."

"It will be better that I don't disturb it then. The doctor is coming in the helicopter and he'll fix it up fine. Oh, hear that sound? They're right above us."

Skye began to gather up the branches that Terry had broken and moved to the opening of the cave. "I'll get a fire going real quickly out here on the ledge and get you warmed up. Then I better scramble back up top and put some flares around that clearing."

"There was some wood in here when I fell, so I had a fire until the wood ran out this morning," Terry said proudly. "I carried a big candle and matches in plastic, like Washington said to do. And I heated some rocks to help keep me and Prince warm. Prince curled around me and helped keep me warm, too. I'm sure glad I brought him."

Skye started a fire and was breaking up small twigs, placing them in it carefully. "You sure used your head," Skye said approvingly. "Why did you bring Prince?"

"I knew he would know the way home if I got lost," Terry said simply. "I had to put a leash on him. He didn't want to go."

"I'm not surprised at that. I am surprised that Prince fell down the cliff, though," Skye said.

"He didn't," Terry said candidly. "I still had him on the leash and when I fell, I pulled him over, too. He fell on my leg and hurt it."

Suddenly remembering his candy bar and Terry's probable need for some quick energy, Skye reached into the pocket of his coat. His hand touched a lumpy, fuzzy object. Bringing it out into the dim light of the flashlight still lying in the cave, Skye held out Terry's stuffed dog.

"Say, I found Sparky back up the stream," he said. "That's how I happened to think you might be near the stream." He turned the bedraggled toy over in his hands and found a rip in the side. "I see that Sparky needs some repairs." He stuck a long, exploring finger inside the rip. "I'll have Washington add some cotton to him and sew up the tear."

"That's okay," Terry said. "That rip has been there for a long time. I don't care if he's torn."

But suddenly Skye was not listening. His probing fingers had felt something in the body and he pulled out a piece of paper. Puzzled, he squinted at it in the dim light. His heart lurched as he made out a word on the bottom of the crumpled piece of paper — *Lillian!*

With fingers that were unexpectedly unsteady, Skye moved to pick up the flashlight. This was the lost note Lillian had left for him!

With the fire burning steadily, Skye crouched back down under the ledge, oblivious to almost everything else.

Terry moved so he could scan the letter over Skye's arm and let out an exclamation of amazement, "Mamma's letter! I hid it in Sparky! It's been there all the time and I didn't know it!"

In reluctant anxiety, Skye quickly read the brief message. The words were badly scribbled and ran uphill as if written in a hurry by an unsteady hand.

"*Skye, I'm going away with Bob. He loves me and wants to marry me. I once loved you, but I must have more than your constant condemnation. I'm leaving Terry with you. I love him and will visit him when I can, but a boy needs his father. And Terry is your son. Contrary to what you believe, I have never been unfaithful to you. Please don't hate me. Lillian*"

Suddenly Terry spoke almost matter-of-factly, "I guess Mamma left us both, didn't she?"

"Yes, I guess she did, Terry," Skye replied in a shaky, husky voice. "But we've still got a lot of living to do, haven't we? Lillian has been gone for three years. Let's leave her in the grave and get on with our lives. What do you say?"

Terry searched Skye's face solemnly for a long moment. "Let's," he agreed quietly.

The fire was crackling cheerfully now, and at Prince's sharp bark, the whirring sound of a helicopter reminded Skye that there were other things that must be done. The chatter of the blades in the cold night air sounded comfortably close and loud.

"I've got to get up there and put out those flares," Skye said quickly. He saw fear flash into Terry's pinched face. Putting his hand on Terry's shoulder, he

286

said gently, "Don't worry, I won't be gone long and Prince will be here with you. You've been incredibly brave, Terry, and I'm *very* proud of you. Can you be my brave son for a few more minutes?"

Terry gulped, then locked his trusting eyes with his father's and nodded his head.

Skye gave his shoulder a quick squeeze, picked up the flashlight and moved quickly to the knotted nylon rope dangling in front of the cave. In minutes he was putting out flares in the tiny clearing not far from the ledge. The helicopter which had been hovering above the treetops over the lone flare Skye had put out earlier, came swiftly down and settled upon the crusted snow as soon as the flares outlined the site.

Jeffrey climbed out and immediately began to unload a stretcher and ropes. "How's the boy?" he called.

"Exhausted, I think, and chilled to the bone. His leg is fractured just above the ankle, I'm afraid. But he's fortunate to be alive. You brought a stretcher?"

"That we did," Dr. Hestley replied, climbing stiffly from the helicopter with a black bag in his hand. "And also some medical supplies. Now, if you'll just lead the way, we'll see what we can do for that boy of yours."

The three men moved swiftly to the ledge above Terry. Skye slid down the rope and was helping to lower the stretcher when Washington came into the clearing on the snowmobile. After the doctor and Jeffrey had gone down the side of the cliff on the rope, Washington followed.

Dr. Hestley seemed almost curt with the adults, but with Terry he was gentle and reassuring. "We have to move you but I'm giving you a shot so it won't hurt. Okay?" At Terry's hesitant nod, he grinned. "Close your eyes, hold your breath and it won't even hurt."

Terry obediently closed his eyes and almost before he had time to draw in his breath, the doctor had deftly inserted and emptied the needle.

"Now," the doctor said, "drink a cup of this hot chocolate while the shot takes effect. It'll warm you up." He poured out a cup of steaming liquid and handed it to Terry.

Terry took a swallow of the chocolate and then spied Washington. He grinned. "Hi, Washington. I remembered all you told me about survival," he said proudly. "Prince and I haven't even been too hungry. I brought raisins, dried apricots, jerky, almonds and candy bars." His voice was growing drowsy. "I-even-brought-a-compass — but-I-forgot-how-to-use-it," he said ruefully.

Washington glanced apprehensively at Skye before he answered heartily, "You're a sharp kid, all right."

"He's my son," Skye said emphatically with a big grin. "Naturally he's sharp."

Terry's eyes had closed but as his ears caught those words, his eyes snapped open again. A warm light glowed there. "I'm Daddy's real son," he said. And his eyes closed.

31

But back at Windthorn, more than ominous clouds had drawn in around Joy. About the time Skye found Terry's little brown toy dog, Joy was alone at Windthorn. Two women from the resort had been with her part of the day helping to make sandwiches, brownies and coffee for the searchers. But when Jeffrey had come in the helicopter for the last of the food at about three o'clock, the ladies had departed with him. After the food was dropped off at the designated places, he had flown the women back to the resort. In the evening, when Kim arrived to relieve her, Joy was to call Jeffrey on the radio and he would come for her.

Alone now, Joy cleaned the kitchen and then went to the library and tried to read. But she couldn't keep her mind on a book with Terry alone in that wintry wilderness and night coming on again. Restless, she wandered out of the library and down to the kitchen, found an apple and moved desultorily back toward the library.

A sound from upstairs caught her attention. Her heart leaped with hope! Could it be Terry?

Swiftly and silently she sped up the stairs. Hesitating at the head of the stairway, she listened intently. There it was again! The sound was muffled but someone was definitely in the room Joy had occupied while staying here — Terry's mother's room.

Joy moved softly across the hall to the door of Lillian's room. Gently she turned the doorknob and pushed inward. The door opened without a sound and Joy eased into the room. Her eyes swept the interior — and widened as she saw the figure standing with his back to her. It was not Terry but Kim! What was he doing here instead of out searching with the others?

Stunned, Joy watched as he removed the little metal diamonds from the back of the waterfall picture which was lying face down on a small table. A sudden, inexplicable fear prickled down her back and she tried to retreat from the room without being seen.

But she must have made a small sound because Kim whirled about. In one hand he held a pocketknife that he had been using to extract the metal brads. The sharp tip was pointed directly at her.

Butterflies of alarm were fluttering in her stomach, but Joy forced herself to speak naturally. "Hi, Kim. I didn't mean to startle you, but I heard someone up here and thought perhaps Terry had returned."

For a long tense moment Kim looked at her without a word. His handsome face did not carry his usual shy smile. The dark, dark eyes glittered cold and hard as obsidian.

When he didn't speak, Joy began to back out the door again. "Sorry I disturbed you," she said nervously.

"Stop!" The flat voice held a deadly menace. Kim's well-chiseled lips curled into a sneer. "Since you are here, perhaps you can be useful to me. Come in and close the door."

As Joy hesitated, Kim deftly flipped the knife in his hand and poised to throw it. "I-I don't understand, Kim. W-what do you want of me," she queried as she slowly stepped back into the room and even more slowly closed the door. Her mind was reeling. Could this be Kim? Shy, smiling, helpful Kim? The change in him was bewildering — and frightening.

Kim ignored her question. "Sit there," he ordered brusquely, indicating an ornate, straight chair.

Joy slid into it. Her heart was pounding with terror and she felt slightly nauseous. What would Kim do to her?

Kim turned his back on her, walked to a large chest of drawers and began to rummage in the drawers.

Seizing the momentary chance, Joy leaped to her feet and fled to the door. She had it open and was out in the hall before Kim realized what was happening. But she hadn't gone a dozen flying steps when Kim's strong brown hand grabbed her arm, yanking her to a sudden halt.

Turning her to face him, she saw his face twist with fury. Releasing her arms, he clamped both hands about her throat.

Dear God, help me! The cry came from her heart but not her lips as Kim's strong fingers shut off her air. Terrified, she struggled and fought with all her strength. The pressure on her throat inexorably tightened. Her breath became ragged, black spots danced before her eyes and consciousness began to drain from her body.

She sagged and would have fallen but Kim released his hold on her throat and caught her. She drew in an agonized, rasping breath as oxygen flowed back into her starving lungs. Gasping and coughing, she gradually regained her breath and equilibrium then stood swaying on trembly legs.

Kim half pulled, half dragged her back into the room and pushed her roughly onto the chair again. He stepped away and stood glaring malevolently at her.

"Don't try that again or I'll finish what I started, right now," he growled.

"Why, Kim? Why are you angry with me? What have I done?" the words burst from her lips of their own volition.

Kim's laugh was bitter. "Just being a rich American is enough," he said enigmatically. Moving with the lithe, fluid grace of a big cat in the wilds, he crossed to the bureau again and with his back to her, swiftly searched through the top drawer.

I think he'd be glad if I gave him an excuse to carry out his threat, Joy thought in horror. She had no doubts now that Kim was capable of killing her.

Kim returned to her chair with a nylon hose. For a terrifying moment, Joy thought he planned to strangle her with it. But instead, he pulled her arms behind her back and lashed them tightly behind the chair-back.

Without another word, Kim strode to the small table and resumed the task of removing the small metal pins from the waterfall picture.

Joy's throat still throbbed from the pressure of Kim's cruel, vice-like fingers and it felt raw and swollen. She tried not to think how close she had come to death just minutes before. *What is going on here?* she thought, her whole body pulsing with apprehension.

When the metal brads had been removed, Kim carefully lifted off the heavy cardboard back. Before Joy's startled eyes, Kim tenderly — almost reverently — drew out a faded, ragged-edged piece of aged leather. Skye's missing, ancient scroll! How had it gotten into the picture? It hadn't been there when Skye took the back from the picture the day they discovered it missing.

Joy must have gasped audibly because Kim looked up and chuckled gleefully. "Yes, Missus Kyle, I'm the one who stole the scroll!"

"But why, Kim? Skye has been good to you. He took you off the streets of Hawaii and brought you into his own home and gave you a good job. Why would you do this to Skye?"

A murderous gleam glazed Kim's obsidian eyes. "Oh, yes," he said mockingly, "Mr. Windthorn has been very good to me! He brought me home and made me his servant!"

"B-but it is no disgrace to be a servant," Joy protested. "And I'm sure he has paid you well."

"I am descended from a noble line in Hawaii," Kim said haughtily. "Yet I have been given the place of a serf — the menial tasks of an attendant. But I have done my work well," the voice was cold, unemotional, "and bided my time."

"You've *planned* to steal this rare scroll?"

Kim's quick laugh was contemptuous. "For a very long time. Not necessarily this scroll, but I knew if I waited long enough, something of priceless value would fall into my hands. And it has! I already have a buyer who is eagerly awaiting this little treasure." He lightly caressed the scroll as if it were a living thing.

"But why would a rich collector buy something he could never display?" Joy asked. "Something rare like this would be immediately recognized as stolen."

"There are those who do not care that the world will never know they possess a treasure such as this. Their pleasure is in knowing they possess it."

"You can't get away with this, Kim," Joy said with spirit. "When you disappear, Skye will know you took the scroll. The police will find you before you're out of Idaho."

Kim's laugh had an unpleasant ring. "Oh, I'm not going to disappear, you are!"

Joy felt as though the breath had been knocked from her. "Me? Wh-what do you mean?"

Kim's narrowed eyes were slits of malice. "I had first planned to frame Terry for the theft. I even took the marble statue from Mr. Windthorn's desk and planted it in Terry's room twice to set the stage for the boy stealing the scroll! But since you so obligingly came up here and caught me with my prize, you will do just as well."

"You didn't harm Terry?" Joy asked in quick alarm.

"No, I had nothing to do with his disappearance. But my guess is that the weakling will be frozen into an icicle when he is found!" he said callously. "It would have been easy to lay the theft on a corpse that can't defend itself!" Kim's laugh held sadistic glee.

"B-but I thought you liked Terry. You were patient and kind with him."

"I hated every minute of waiting on that spoiled brat!" Kim said savagely.

Stunned by his ferocity, Joy couldn't keep a tremor from her low voice as she asked, "W-what are you going to do with me?"

Kim grinned wickedly, obviously enjoying the power he held over her. "Maybe I'll let you choose the path of your departure from this fair earth!"

When her face paled and panic leaped into her expressive face, he chuckled. Then suddenly he sobered and his eyes narrowed dangerously. "Enough of this! I've lost enough time because of you. I wouldn't advise you to try to get away. I'll be back in a minute, and then we can be on our way." He strode abruptly from the room.

As soon as Kim left the room, though, Joy began to twist her hands in their bonds, frantically straining against the strong nylon hose that held her until her wrists felt chafed and raw. After a couple of minutes, she realized it was hopeless.

Joy looked wildly about the room. Kim would be back any minute. If only there was something here to help her to escape!

The knife! It was lying on top of the picture. Maybe she could reach it!

She put her feet solidly on the floor and

raised herself and the chair awkwardly. But she had only taken a couple of tiny steps when she heard Kim's footsteps in the hallway. The despair in her throat was a bitter gorge to swallow as she sat back down.

"Father, help me," she whispered as Kim came back into the room. Calmness, like a pleasant warmth, started somewhere deep inside her and spread through her body. God was with her. She relaxed against the chair.

Kim scarcely glanced at her as he crossed the room. He carried the thin case that housed the scroll.

Kim is doing this thing in style, she thought as she watched him place the scroll in its protective case. *He is even stealing the case it came in!*

"Kim," Joy said, "it was you who tampered with the picture while I was here, wasn't it?"

Kim's white teeth showed in a broad sneer. "I hung the picture crooked to make you notice it; then I took it away and later returned it."

"Why?" Joy pretended to give Kim her whole attention while she twisted her hands trying to reach the ring her father had given her a few months ago for her birthday. It was a delicate ring set with rubies and diamonds surrounding a very large diamond which she deeply treasured.

Pride in his own cunning shone in Kim's face. "I stole the scroll and hid it in a dark corner on a top shelf in your closet. After all, if it were found, I didn't plan for it to ever be connected to me! I knew you would connect the disappearance of the picture from your room, and its return, with the theft of the scroll.

"And of course you did," he gloated, "and suggested to Mr. Windthorn that he check the picture. Naturally it wasn't there."

Joy had the ring between the fingers of her other hand now, and very gently eased it off. She felt it drop and hoped fervently that it had landed under her chair.

"If you recall," Kim continued, "Mr. Windthorn ordered me to put the picture back together again. I went after a tool to give everyone time to leave. When I got back, it took only a few seconds to get the scroll and hide it in the picture as I had planned. Once the picture was searched, it was unlikely to be searched again. Clever, wasn't it?"

"Yes, very," Joy said. If she could only keep him talking and bragging, maybe —

just maybe — someone would return. "So you plan to stay on here working for Skye even after you have sold the scroll?" she asked.

"For awhile, until there is no danger that the theft will be connected with me. Then I'm going to be homesick for Hawaii. Everyone knows I've been saving for a trip there for a couple of years." He chuckled suddenly. "What they don't know is that I have a whole cache of jewels and money in a safety deposit box to add to my savings when I leave!"

Stunned astonishment shone in Joy's face as his words triggered a sudden realization. "You're the Midnight Cat Burglar!" she exclaimed. "B-but how could you have known who had jewels and money in their homes?"

"I've dated a few of the girls who worked at the resort and in some of the mansions around here. You'd be surprised how a few soft words will loosen a girl's tongue!"

"And when you get to Hawaii, you don't plan to come back?"

"Right! When I get there, I'll find a job and tell Mr. Windthorn I liked my homeland so well I decided to stay. Mr. Windthorn will understand. He's always been very kind to me," he said with a sneer.

Abruptly Kim sobered. He crossed to the picture and swiftly replaced a few metal brads to hold the back in place. Gathering up the other metal diamonds, he dumped them in the little table drawer and pocketed the knife. Then he moved swiftly to Joy, untied her wrists, and pulled her roughly to her feet.

"Come on over here," he said, propelling her across the room to the picture. He carefully wiped every inch of the picture with a large dust cloth. "Now," he ordered, "pick up the picture and turn it over."

"You want me to put my fingerprints on the picture," Joy said aghast. "They'll think I'm guilty. I won't!"

Kim's lips twisted with anger. "*Won't*, Mrs. Kyle?" His voice was soft and threatening. His hand again held the small knife.

Fear lanced through Joy's body and she quickly did as she was told. He ordered her to place her fingers as if she were removing the metal diamonds and she reluctantly obeyed. When she had finished, Kim ordered her to hang the picture.

"Now you must leave Mr. Windthorn a note," Kim said. He produced stationery and a pen from the drawer of the little table and handed them to Joy. "Tell him you started feeling bad and decided to go back to the resort early."

"But that's a lie and I won't write it!"

Kim's lips twisted into an evil grin and his dark eyes glittered. His words were almost a hiss. "You will be very sick — and soon — if you don't do my bidding!"

In sick despair Joy took the pen and wrote the brief note. *It isn't a lie,* Joy thought, *now I do feel sick.*

"We'll leave it on the kitchen table," Kim said after he had read the note with obvious satisfaction.

Kim's eyes raked the room and stopped as he noticed the hose lying on the floor near the chair. Joy held her breath as he walked over and stooped to pick it up. Her heart plummeted to her toes when she saw his hand move away from the hose and close upon her ring.

Kim's eyes glittered with greed as he held the jeweled ring in the palm of his brown hand. He flicked a glance at Joy. "I suppose you meant for Mr. Windthorn to find this. It *is* a beauty, but since you won't be needing it, I'll just be its little guardian!" He touched it lightly with his lips and dropped it in a trouser pocket.

"Have you ever used snowshoes?" Kim asked abruptly.

"A long time ago, as a teenager," Joy admitted grudgingly.

"Good. There are several pair in the garage and that's how we're leaving."

"Leaving? W-where are we going?"

"No more questions," Kim said testily. "Come on downstairs, get your snow gear on and we'll be going."

A few minutes later Joy and Kim, dressed for the outdoors, were on snowshoes and headed into the deep forest behind Windthorn. Kim carried the scroll case, covered in heavy plastic, in a light backpack.

As they topped a rise, Joy looked back. She had been glancing back every few minutes of the strenuous climb, hoping someone would arrive at Windthorn to help her. But with a leaden heart, she saw no movement or sound. Kim grabbed her arm and shoved her ahead of him.

Father God, she cried out silently as she stumbled and almost fell, *where are you?*

All around her was the empty desolation of deep snow, bitter cold and dense forest. And night was coming rapidly. Was she going to die out here? What horrible death had Kim planned for her?

Suddenly Joy brought her thoughts up short. *Joy,* she told herself sternly, *even if you are about to die you can meet it with a clear head and with dignity. God is with you whether you live or die. Reach for Him. He's there!*

New strength seemed to flow into her body as she imagined reaching out her hand and placing it in God's hand.

But the travel was still rough. She hadn't been on snowshoes in many years and this was some of the roughest country she had ever encountered. She fell repeatedly as she tried to maneuver the awkward snowshoes. It seemed that every muscle of her body was soon aching from the grueling pace Kim set as they struggled over the rough, snow covered terrain.

Once she stumbled into a narrow crevasse and was enveloped in the snow. It wasn't deep, but as she clawed her way out, Kim watched with his arms crossed and a derisive smirk on his face. After she struggled out, he shoved her down the slope ahead of him.

Soon her legs felt like lead and her breath was coming in raspy gasps. But Kim forced her on. Finally, she stumbled and fell into a snowbank — and could not get up. Her head was ringing and Kim's angry voice seemed far away. Her limbs felt weighted and her lungs were on fire as she lay gasping for breath.

When Kim could not prod or threaten her into rising, he grudgingly brushed the snow from a log and sat down to rest, too. He was also breathing hard. He drew out a candy bar, peeled back the cover and began to eat.

When Joy had regained her breath, Kim carelessly tossed her a candy bar. She sat up, tore off the wrapper and ate it greedily. When she had finished it, Kim hauled her to her feet and from somewhere deep within she found the strength to move forward.

A short while later Kim gave Joy a tiny breather when he stopped at a ledge of rock. She sank down gratefully on the snow while he pushed the plastic wrapped scroll case far back in a hole under the rock. Then he carefully piled the snow back over the opening and smoothed it out until there was no sign it had been disturbed.

He doesn't plan for me to come back alive or he would not have hidden that case where I could see him, Joy thought dully. She was so tired that even this thought seemed unreal and nightmarish.

Kim rose from hiding the scroll, yanked Joy to her feet, and they moved off again.

By now the sun had sunk behind the treetops and darkness was rapidly settling over the snowy hillsides. They came into a small clearing, and through the gathering gloom, Joy looked ahead, then drew back in alarm. A few feet in front of them the ground fell sharply away.

Kim forced her forward and she saw a nearly vertical, snow covered slope before them. It looked like an avalanche must have at some time swept it clear of trees; only a few scattered boulders were visible on the steep expanse of snow.

Kim was staring down the incline.

"We aren't going to try to go down that slope, are we?" Joy asked fearfully.

Kim turned to look at her in the fading light. Though dark, there was still enough illumination for her to see that he was smiling — an evil smile that caused her to shrink away from him.

"No. No, *we* aren't going down," he said softly. "Take off your snowshoes!"

Although shaking with fear, Joy considered refusing, but Kim's hard, cruel eyes convinced her to do as ordered. Removing her mittens, she clumsily loosened the binding on the snowshoes and handed them to Kim.

Kim placed his knee in the middle of

one of the snowshoes and twisted it. Then he threw it and its mate far down the slope.

Joy started to draw the mittens back on her rapidly chilling fingers but Kim snatched them away and threw them down the hillside after the snowshoes.

Joy lifted unflinching eyes to Kim's face. "What are you going to do, let me freeze to death?"

Kim laughed, low and ugly, and then slowly, as if savoring his words, said, "I'm going to break your neck and throw you down there." He motioned toward the steep slope. "Everyone will think you got turned around and couldn't find your way back to the resort. You fell down the mountain in the dark and broke your neck! A snowshoe was broken and you lost your mittens as you tumbled down."

Joy drew in her breath sharply.

Kim laughed softly again. "I always wondered what it would be like to break a human neck with my bare hands. I once broke a dog's neck in Hawaii when it attacked me in an alley. I never forgot the thrill!"

Kim took a step toward her and Joy took a step backward. Fearfully she thought, *Kim is really going to kill me!* "Kim," she said through trembling lips, "no human is here, but God sees what you are doing. You can't hide from Him."

Kim looked startled, then threw up his head and laughed. "I'm not afraid of the God of the rich Americans," he hooted.

Suddenly a strange feeling came over Joy. A curious calmness accompanied the unfolding of every sense as they seemed to come tinglingly alive and alert. She would not stand passively still while Kim killed her!

She saw Kim's strong brown hands whip toward her neck. She darted sideways out of his reach, using her one small advantage. The snow was only lightly crusted here and Kim was wearing bearpaw snowshoes and she was not. He could not move about as freely as she.

He grabbed for her once more and she sprang away again. Kim sucked in his breath, cursed savagely, and lunged for her. She dodged away but one hard, brown hand gripped her arm. She swung around and slashed at his face with stiff fingers. Deep red scratches appeared on one side of Kim's face.

The next few minutes, Joy fought Kim like a tigress. With every ounce of her strength, she used teeth, feet, fists and raking nails. She fought and dodged, desperately trying to keep those powerfully cruel hands from closing on her throat.

Kim swore as he struggled to get a stranglehold on her throat. Finally, he struck her a stunning blow on the side of her head with his fist.

Blinding pain arched through Joy's head and she felt herself falling. She tried to catch herself but she struck the ground with a painful jar. Then she was rolling . . . rolling . . . rolling.

As if in slow motion her benumbed mind registered what had happened. Kim's blow had sent her over the edge and she was rolling down the mountainside! She threw up her arms to protect her face.

Gathering speed as she rolled, Joy felt the sting of brush on her partly exposed face and the painful jars as her body bounced over little washes, hidden rocks and other obstructions. A small tree trunk slowed her plunging fall, then bent and let her continue rolling down the steep slope.

Joy felt as if she had been rolling for an eternity. Her body was one throbbing ache. The jarring knocked away her breath and she was dizzy from the continuous motion.

She was near the bottom when suddenly her body struck a large, snow shrouded rock. A searing pain ran down her shoulder and side. She tried to cry out, but the wind ripped the words away. She fought to remain conscious, but blackness rushed to envelop her. Then merciful darkness reached out and swallowed her.

32

Skye was heating stew on the big gas range when Kim entered the kitchen from the garage.

"Terry's home safely!" he greeted his houseboy exuberantly.

"That's great!" Kim said, his dark eyes warm, and his white teeth flashing in a big smile. "Is he okay?"

"His leg is fractured but Dr. Hestley doesn't seem to think it's a bad break; he put a cast on it. Terry was so exhausted that he went to sleep even before the doctor left. He's resting like he could sleep 'til next Christmas."

Suddenly Skye looked closely at Kim. "Say, what happened to your face?"

Kim fingered the lacerations on the right side of his face and said easily, "Just slipped and fell into a little gully. No problem, just some scratches."

"You'd better take care of them with an

antiseptic," Skye said. "But why don't you have some of this stew first. It's hot, and you look beat."

"Thanks, I'd like to," Kim said. "I'm starved."

He gathered up a bowl, cup and silverware and sat down at the kitchen table just as they heard Washington call from the front of the house.

"We're in the kitchen," Skye called, "come on in and have some hot stew."

"How's Terry?" Washington asked as soon as he entered the room.

Skye gave him the same report he'd just given Kim.

Washington grinned at Kim as he moved to the table. "Looks like you've been in a battle with a mountain lion."

"Only with the branches of a bush," Kim said ruefully. "I fell in a gully. Guess I'm lucky I didn't get a broken leg."

Skye paused with his spoon in midair. "Did either of you see Mrs. Kyle this afternoon? When we got home she was gone and had left a note that she was going back to the resort since she didn't feel well."

Both men denied seeing Joy.

"Jeffrey and I are quite concerned," Skye said. "It's a long trek to the resort. If she had called Jeffrey on the two-way radio, he would have taken her home as usual."

"She's a real considerate lady," Washington said. "Probably just hated to take anyone away from the search to take her home."

"I suppose," Skye said, "but she didn't even have her skis."

"Maybe she borrowed some of the snow-shoes from the garage," Kim said quickly. "I'll go see if any are missing." He was back almost immediately. "There is a pair gone."

"Joy must have taken off on snowshoes then," Skye mused. "But it seems so odd for her to try such a thing all alone."

"Yes, it does," agreed Washington.

"Well, we should know soon if Joy got there all right," Skye said. "Jeffrey took Dr. Hestley home in the helicopter and he's to call as soon as he gets there."

Just as he finished speaking, the two-way radio lying in the middle of the table came to life and Skye snatched it up.

"Skye," Jeffrey said abruptly, "Joy didn't show up here at the resort. The Lorings and I are really worried. We're afraid she got lost on the way. Carole was amazed that Joy would even try to come to Forest Lakes by herself; she didn't really know the way."

"The whole thing is a puzzle. Joy seems much too sensible to try something like that," Skye said worriedly.

"Also," Jeffrey's words crackled over the radio, "I wasn't convinced Joy wrote that note because it would have been so easy to call, so I brought it over to Carole. She said it looks like Joy's handwriting but that the signature wasn't right."

"What do you mean?" Skye asked in alarm.

"Carole declares that Joy would never have signed her name 'Mrs. Ferron Kyle.' Joy's late husband's name is so repugnant to Joy that she never even says it unless she has to!"

"I guess I didn't notice it was signed that way," Skye said. "This is all rather strange. There were a lot of men roaming the woods during this search. Surely one of them hasn't harmed Joy. I've been so concerned about Terry that I never dreamed she might be in danger."

"None of us did. Carole says Joy didn't even take her skis. She would never have tried to come back on foot."

"A pair of our snowshoes is missing so we presume she borrowed those. Have you checked with the head ranger to see if any of the searchers saw Joy?"

"Yes, David just did. No one reported seeing her, but the ranger said he would contact the Job Corps people, and other rangers and everyone else who helped in the search.

"I hope we're getting worked up for nothing," Jeffrey said, "and that Joy will come walking in any minute. David, Dr. Hestley and I are going to make some runs between here and Windthorn with the helicopter. We'll use the searchlight. The chopper can cover a lot more ground more quickly, so why don't you sit tight until we have a good look. Okay?"

"Okay, but I don't think we should wait too long before we get a search party underway. It's going to be cold out there tonight."

"Right! We'll keep in touch. Over and out."

"Sir," Washington said as Skye laid the radio down. "I think you had better finish your supper. This could be a long night again. I'll reheat it, if you would like."

"No, that's fine." He picked up a spoon and began to eat hurriedly.

"Mr. Windthorn," Kim spoke up, "I have a thought that you should consider. Isn't there a possibility that Mrs. Kyle is not what she appears? And that she stole your rare scroll and has escaped with it?"

Both Skye and Washington stared at Kim in dumb amazement. Washington recovered first. "That's absurd, Kim!"

Kim looked slightly flustered but continued, "It may not be as ridiculous as you think. I thought about this out in the woods today. We all know that neither you or I took it. Mrs. Loring was in bed with her bad knee and Terry denies taking it. That only leaves Mrs. Kyle. She had the free run of the place and who would suspect a pretty young woman from a wealthy family?"

As Kim talked, incredulity had spread across Skye's face. "I could never believe Joy would steal that scroll!"

"That's just the point, boss. None of us would. But the scroll is missing."

"Much as I don't want to, maybe we should at least examine Kim's idea," Washington said thoughtfully. "I don't like the idea either but that scroll did disappear during the short time the ladies were here."

"But why did Joy come back if she stole the scroll?" Skye said stubbornly. "And what would this have to do with her disappearance now?"

Kim shrugged expressively. "Maybe she was afraid she might be caught if she took it away before, so she hid the scroll and had to come back to get it. Remember, she was the one who asked to come here and relieve Washington so he could help in the search. I heard her."

"I just don't think it's possible that Joy is a thief," Skye reiterated.

Kim shrugged indifferently. "It was just a thought."

"It would have been too risky for Joy to hide the scroll in the house," Skye continued as if Kim hadn't spoken. "She wouldn't know I would invite her back."

"Pretty girls like that could find a way," Kim said.

"It could have been hidden outside," Washington suggested.

"No," Skye was shaking his head. "She never went outside; it was storming the whole time she was here."

"Maybe she hid it in the room she stayed in," Kim suggested. "She could have retrieved it today and taken off. Maybe there was a partner waiting to pick her up."

Kim snapped his fingers excitedly, "Mr. Windthorn, I know where the ideal place to hide it would be, if she did take the scroll. Behind that waterfall picture! Remember? She had you check there for it? What better place to hide it than a place that had already been searched!"

"It wouldn't hurt to check," Washington urged.

Skye got up reluctantly. "I pray to God you aren't right," he said as if he were talking to himself.

When they entered Lillian's old room, Skye went swiftly to the picture. Taking it down, he turned it over. Washington and Kim crowded close to see.

"Most of the pins are gone!" Washington exclaimed.

"Whoever took this apart probably left fingerprints all over it," Washington said thoughtfully.

"A professional thief wouldn't leave fingerprints," Skye said.

"But Mrs. Kyle might not be a professional," Kim said. "She could have just realized how rare and valuable the scroll was and taken advantage of the opportunity."

Washington stared at Kim, then asked suddenly, "Were you back at the house any time this afternoon, Kim?"

"No, I wasn't," Kim declared. "When I left you early this afternoon, I headed away from the house. Why do you ask?"

Washington looked at Kim with fathomless black eyes until Kim flushed slightly and said irritably, "Why are you staring at me?"

"Because you're lying," Washington stated flatly. "You were at the house this afternoon."

Kim's face flushed a deep red as he sputtered, "How dare you accuse me of lying!"

Skye's face expressed bewilderment as he stared at Washington. "What makes you think Kim was at the house this afternoon?"

"When Kim left me early today, he was using cross-country skis and was headed west. When he came back home tonight, he came in from the north and was wearing snowshoes."

"That's a lie!" Kim almost shouted.

"And it appears to me that Kim is very anxious to indict Mrs. Kyle for the theft of the scroll." Washington paused, then finished softly, "Maybe you are the thief, Kim."

Kim seemed to straighten with a great effort. He turned to Skye. "Sir, I don't know why Washington would accuse me of taking your scroll, but I'm not guilty and I refuse to stand here and be insulted. You know I have always been loyal to you in every way."

Skye looked from Kim to Washington and back again. Then he spoke peremptorily to Washington. "Are you sure you saw

320

Kim return from the north on snow-shoes?"

Washington turned to Skye. "I accidentally stalled the snowmobile about a half mile from here a while ago. It wouldn't start again so I left it and came home on foot. I was coming into our clearing when I saw a light coming from the north and thought it might be a prowler, so I stepped back into the trees and waited.

"When the figure moved into the back-yard, I saw that he was on snowshoes. I couldn't see who it was. As you probably noticed, there is a moon tonight but it isn't very bright."

Skye was listening silently, his face in-scrutable. Kim was staring at Washington as if hypnotized.

"When he got to that old tool shed, I saw the figure go in," Washington continued. "I slipped out of the woods and hurried as fast and as silently as I could to the back of the shed."

Washington turned to Kim. "And when the man came out a few minutes later and started to the house, I could see under the mercury light that it was you! The snow-shoes were gone and you had your skis over your shoulder.

"I couldn't figure out why you didn't

want anyone to know you had been on snowshoes. So I waited until you went into the house and then went around to the front and came in that way."

The eyes of both Skye and Washington were on Kim. Kim glared at Washington and then turned to Skye. "You don't believe that crazy story? It's his word against mine."

"Only mine can be proven," Washington said calmly. "I looked in the shed. The snowshoes are there for anyone to see, still wet and snowy like they were when you took them off."

"Okay! So I did come home and change to snowshoes. What of it?" Kim questioned belligerently. "That doesn't prove I took the scroll."

"Do you have an explanation, Kim?" Skye asked, his voice grim.

Kim swallowed hard. "There's nothing deep or dark about it. I just decided I might do better with snowshoes than with skis so I came home to change. I hated to admit it because I was afraid you'd think I was shirking on the job by taking time out to come home."

"You didn't see Joy?" Skye asked.

"Of course not!" Kim had regained his composure. "I don't know if she was still here or not. I just went into the garage and got some snowshoes."

"Why so secretive then?" Washington said. "You acted like you didn't want anyone to know you had been wearing snowshoes."

"I wasn't hiding anything. I left my skis in the tool shed and put the snowshoes on at the house, then I walked to the tool shed to try them out. I hadn't used snowshoes in a long time and I wasn't sure how they would feel on my feet," Kim said smoothly.

"Then if you aren't guilty of any wrongdoing, you shouldn't mind if we search you or your room," Skye said slowly.

Anger flashed in Kim's eyes, "I'll not submit to such an indignity!" he said heatedly.

"I'm afraid I must insist," Skye said firmly. "If you're not guilty, we'll owe you an apology. Search him, Washington."

Before Washington could move, Kim turned and dashed from the room. Both men charged after him and caught him just as he reached the stairway.

Kim's face was livid with rage and his eyes were pools of hot anger. Washington held his struggling body while Skye searched him, running his hands quickly over his clothes. Suddenly Skye said,

"There's something in this pocket."

Kim swore savagely and nearly broke free. For a minute it took both Skye and Washington to hold him. Washington finally pinioned Kim's arms behind him with powerful hands, and Skye reached into Kim's pocket to draw out the object it contained.

A ring lay in the palm of Skye's hand, its diamonds and rubies flashing fire in the hall light!

"Where did you get this?" Skye demanded. His eyes had gone as cold as black ice; his voice was grim and harsh.

"I found it in the woods this afternoon and it's mine!" Kim said angrily.

Skye's stern gaze dropped back to the jeweled ring blinking in his hand. He turned it between his fingers. When he looked back at Kim, his eyes blazed with carefully controlled anger. "What did you do with Joy?"

"I-I don't know what you're talking about," Kim blustered.

Skye took a step toward Kim and his voice was deadly quiet. "This ring belongs to Joy Kyle. She was wearing it yesterday!"

Kim swallowed hard. "I don't know where she is. I told you I found the ring today — in the woods. Maybe she lost it there."

"No more lies! What have you done with her?" Skye took another step toward Kim and he backed away. Skye's face was pale as death, his lips a thin line, compressed with wrath, his eyes pools of smoldering rage.

"Those scratches on your face were not made by brush. Someone raked your face with sharp fingernails! And I think they were Joy's! What did you do with her?!"

Kim's hostile obsidian eyes met Skye's briefly and then he kicked viciously backward, striking Washington's leg a brutal blow with his boot heel. Caught off guard, Washington released his hold and staggered back, his face twisted with pain. Kim sprang clear and fled down the stairs.

Thrusting the ring in his pocket, Skye flew after him, catching him at the foot of the stairway. His fingers were not gentle as they twisted Kim's arm behind his back.

"Where is Joy? Tell me!" Skye thundered.

Kim's voice became a desperate whine, "Mr. Windthorn, I admit that I took the scroll. It's unharmed and I'll return it to you, but I don't know anything about that girl."

"Where did you get her ring?"

"Like I told you — in the woods."

Washington limped down the stairs, grabbed Kim by the front of his shirt, and hauled him up onto his toes. Washington's dark eyes bored into Kim's as he grated out, "Tell me where that sweet little girl is before I break you apart!"

Kim struggled to break free of Washington but Skye held him securely. Bringing his face close to Kim's, Washington demanded savagely, "Where is she?"

Suddenly Kim's face crumpled and his body sagged as he began to blubber, "Okay — okay. I do know where she is. But if she's dead, I didn't kill her! She — she fell down the slope."

Washington shook him. "Was she alive when you last saw her?"

"I-I don't know," Kim muttered. "It was too dark and too far down to tell."

"Didn't you even go down and see?" Skye asked aghast.

In defeat, Kim dumbly shook his head no.

"Where is she?" Washington demanded.

"At the foot of Avalanche Ridge," Kim's voice had sunk to a reluctant whisper.

Releasing Kim's arms, Skye sprinted down the hall to the kitchen. Grabbing the two-way radio, he was speaking to Jeffrey within a minute.

"Jeffrey, get over here quick! We know where Joy is. She's probably badly injured —" Skye's voice faltered, "— or worse. Every minute could count. I can show you better than tell you where she is. I'll be out on the lawn. Please hurry."

33

Joy was in a semiconscious state when she heard the helicopter circling above her. She had been drifting in and out of consciousness ever since her fall down the steep slope. Disoriented, chilled, and rarely completely lucid, pain held her body in a wracking grip. If she moved, it became unbearable and she blacked out.

In her few clear moments she prayed, and tried to keep the hood of her coat drawn over her face with her hands tucked inside the coat as the night cold stole her body heat.

Now Joy was not sure if the sound of the helicopter was real until its blinding searchlight swept over her. She clenched her eyes tightly against its harsh, white glare. Then the light shifted away to her right and she could feel the strong wind the helicopter generated as it settled near her.

She wanted desperately to keep her eyes

open but she found it impossible. She was so tired, so very tired. And the pain! Her body seemed to pulse to the beat of the pain.

She was dimly aware of running footsteps and then a warm hand was on her face, pushing back her hair.

Joy forced open her eyes. Skye was bending over her, his eyes a familiar, warm, smoky grey. He lifted her cold right hand, holding it in both of his deliciously warm hands.

"Joy, can you hear me? Are you all right?" In her confused state the voice sounded husky with emotion.

Joy's reply was a faint whisper, "I'm so cold and I hurt — something awful. I . . ." Her eyes closed in spite of herself and her voice trailed away. She felt tears rolling down her face and tried to stem them, then it didn't seem worth the effort.

There were other voices around her now and different sounds: footsteps, the swish and clink of unidentifiable objects, a case snapping open. A strong medicinal odor reached her nostrils as Skye released her hand and helped smooth a heavy blanket over her.

"Little lady," a faintly familiar voice spoke. "I'm Dr. Hestley and I'll give you something to ease the pain, but first, it would help if you can tell me where you hurt."

Joy tried to open her eyes but the lids were just too heavy. It took all her strength to whisper. "My-left-arm-above-the-elbow-and-my-left-side. It-hurts-when-I-breathe. I'm-so-cold. . . ." Her breath was spent; perspiration glistened on her forehead.

"We'll slit the sleeve of your coat so I can give you a shot. Easy now —" Dr. Hestley's voice was kind.

Suddenly Joy gasped as a searing pain ripped through her left side, shoulder and arm. Long fingers of darkness reached out to claim her. She fought them back with all her strength, but the black mantle settled relentlessly over her. Joy's head fell limply to the side.

"Doctor, is she all right?" Skye was hovering over Joy anxiously.

"She's fainted from the pain," Dr. Hestley said. "When I moved her arm, she flinched and moved the rest of her body." His hands explored along Joy's ribs. "She has several broken ribs as well as a broken arm. I just hope she doesn't have some internal injuries or that one of the broken ribs hasn't punctured the lung. She's also suffering from exposure. We can only pray that we reached her in time. I'm going to give her a shot to ease the pain now. Then we can move her, but very carefully."

The flight back to the resort in the helicopter was completed as quickly as possible. Skye sat beside Joy's still body, holding one cold hand as if willing her out of his own vibrant strength not to die.

All night he sat by her side, then left to see his son as morning broke over the mountain tops. There had been no change as the doctor fought to bring her body temperature back up to normal.

Giving his hand a sympathetic squeeze, Carole remained in her place as Skye left. Twice more he came and went as Joy lay oblivious of her friends and the fight to save her life.

When Joy finally opened her eyes, she didn't know where she was. She shifted slightly and winced. Looking down, she saw that her left arm was in a cast. With her right hand she gingerly felt her left side, discovering that her ribs were tightly taped. She was dressed in a loose fitting hospital garment and covered with a blanket.

A trim blonde nurse stood near the window watering an array of plants and flowers. When she turned around and saw

Joy's eyes open, she smiled cheerfully. "Well, our patient is back in the world of the living. I'm Nurse Kelly. How are you feeling?"

"Tired and very sore — all over," Joy said weakly. "Where am I?"

"In the infirmary at the resort," a voice on the other side of the bed replied.

Joy turned her head quickly and winced. "Ouch," she said, "even my silly neck is sore."

Carole was sitting in a big upholstered chair near the bed. She was smiling, but Joy saw dark smudges under her eyes, and her face was pale with fatigue.

"Carole, have you been sitting here ever since they brought me in?" she accused feebly.

"Well, yes," Carole admitted. "But I did sleep a little, this chair is pretty comfortable. You really have given us quite a scare, you know. First you disappeared and then the search party brought you in looking like death itself."

"You should know I'm not that easy to get rid of," Joy said gamely. She smiled and flinched. Touching her face with her right hand, she said, "No wonder it hurts to laugh, my face is scratched. I must look a sight."

"Your face is not only scratched, your left cheekbone is badly bruised and you have a gorgeous black eye. In fact, your whole body is black and blue. You are very blessed of the Lord to be alive, young lady! I hope you know that!"

"How did you find me?"

"Skye and Washington finally got it out of Kim where you were. Skye called Jeffrey on the two-way radio. We were already frantic about you. Jeffrey, David and the doctor left to pick up Skye in the helicopter."

"I only remember Skye — and the doctor," Joy said slowly. "It's very hazy." She started to sit up, gasped and sank back on the pillow, her face pale and set.

The nurse hurried forward, "Mrs. Kyle, you mustn't try to sit up yet. Are you all right?"

After a moment, Joy laughed shakily. "That was a dumb thing to do." Her voice became serious as she slowly turned her head to look at Carole. "I just remembered about Terry. Has he been found?"

"He's home and doing fine. Although his leg is fractured, Dr. Hestley says it isn't a bad break. Skye was here until this morning. Those gorgeous long-stemmed red roses are from him. The equally beautiful pink ones are from Jeffrey. The potted plant is from David and me."

"That was so sweet of you. They're all so lovely."

"Mrs. Kyle," the nurse spoke apologetically, "I think you should get some rest now."

"And you had better get some, too, Carole," Joy said. "You look dead on your feet. How long have I been asleep?"

"The doctor has kept you sedated for almost two days," Carole said. Her face grew solemn as she said softly, "We had quite a struggle keeping you alive the first twenty-four hours. Since then, you've been almost awake a couple of times. Do you remember asking us not to send for your father? No? Well, you said you didn't want to worry him and that they would be back soon anyway." Carole squeezed Joy's hand. "I'm so glad you're alive, awake, and well. I think I will get a little rest now. I'll see you later."

That evening Joy awoke from a light slumber to see Jeffrey at the door. His hazel eyes lit up when he saw Joy's eyes open.

"How're you feeling?" he asked.

"Much better. And thank you so much for the lovely roses and for helping to rescue me!"

"My pleasure. I've been in to see you several times but you were still sedated and that guard dog of a nurse kept running me away," Jeffrey bantered.

"I heard that," Joy's nurse said from the doorway. Her smile at Jeffrey was teasing. "I'm going down the hall but I'll be back in five minutes to send you on your way." Her long gold lashes swept down over sparkling green eyes as she moved away.

Joy laughed gaily. "You seem to have made a hit with Nurse Kelly. She doesn't smile at me like that!"

"Good, if she's making you jealous," Jeffrey said, grinning.

Jeffrey's manner grew serious as he reached for her hand. "Joy, you are becoming more dear to me every day. When I found out you were missing, it was nearly unbearable. I was so afraid I'd lose you. I think I aged ten years."

"You're very sweet," Joy said gently.

"I want you to think more of me than that," Jeffrey said. "Would you give some thought to 'us'?"

Joy's blue eyes misted. "I'm touched and deeply honored, Jeffrey, that you seem to care for me. I care about you, too, but not that way. I value your friendship — but that's all I can give you." She paused as she

335

saw the hurt in his eyes. Reaching out her hand, she said softly, "Jeffrey, I'm sorry. I wish I felt differently."

Jeffrey wrapped her hand in both of his own. "I don't give up easily," he said, "but I suppose I must accept that for now." He bent and touched his lips to her forehead. "I'd better go before Nurse Kelly runs me off."

Joy watched him go with a sad heart. *Dear Jeffrey,* she thought, *how I wish I could love you!*

How strange, but wonderful, too, she mused, *a short while ago I was concerned and praying that I would know what was love and what it was not. Now, suddenly, just as Carole said, I knew that Jeffrey could never be more than a friend to me even though I wanted him to be more.*

Feeling at peace with her decision, she was lying with her eyes closed a few minutes later when she heard Nurse Kelly say quietly, "I'm sorry, but you can't go in right now. Mrs. Kyle is resting."

"I'll wait, then," a deep voice said.

Joy felt her heart give an excited leap and her pulse quickened. Before Nurse Kelly could answer, Joy spoke, "I'm not asleep. Come on in, Skye."

Skye walked to her bed and Joy thought

again what beautiful eyes he had when he wasn't angry. His thin lips curved into a smile and her heart fluttered. *Whoa, Joy,* she told herself firmly, *your Father wouldn't approve of the feeling that Skye is awakening in your heart. He is not a Christian.* An almost physical pain stabbed her at the realization. Dimly she heard Skye speak.

"How are you feeling?"

"Better than I look with my lovely shiner," Joy said. Suddenly she wished that Skye hadn't seen her with her face scratched and bruised. And again she put a restraining halt on her rebellious thoughts. Skye was not for her.

"A black eye and bruises can never hide your beauty," Skye said softly. "I just wish with all my heart that I'd found out what Kim was before he put you through all this!"

An involuntary tremor ran through Joy's body. "Thank you so much for helping to rescue me! Kim meant to kill me!"

"I know," Skye said. "I wake up in the night in a cold chill thinking how near he came to succeeding!"

"Did you get your rare scroll back?"

Skye nodded. "In perfect condition. After Kim began to unravel, he admitted everything — even about the jewels and the

337

money he had stolen. It's hard to imagine our gentle Kim as the Midnight Cat Burglar — and with the heart of a murderer!" Skye took her hand. "I hope you can put this whole ugly nightmare behind you. Kim is in jail and will be for a long, long time."

Joy smiled up at him, fighting the emotional pain her eyes wanted to reveal.

"Your flowers are lovely," she said, withdrawing her hand gently from Skye's grasp. "Roses are my favorite."

"I hoped they would be. Oh, by the way, Terry said to tell you 'hi' and that he was coming to see you as soon as the doctor will let him leave the house."

"Carole told me Terry had been found. I was so relieved! How are things between you two?"

"Great," Skye said warmly, "and I'm trying hard to keep it that way this time! He's a good boy."

Nurse Kelly appeared at the door. "I'm sorry, Mr. Windthorn, but the doctor's orders are only five minutes per visit until Mrs. Kyle gets her strength back."

"Give me a few more minutes — please," Skye turned a pleading smile upon the nurse.

"Very well, five minutes and no more!

Dr. Hestley can be unmistakably firm if his orders aren't followed." She moved away.

Skye turned back to Joy. "Terry told me that you had given him a couple of verses from the Bible, and they kept him from giving up when he realized he was lost and then through the ordeal on that ledge."

Joy looked quickly at Skye. He didn't seem displeased. "Those verses have helped me many times," she said quietly.

"You are quite a little preacher. Did you know that?" Skye's grey eyes were grave.

Joy was suddenly flustered. She didn't know if Skye was serious or if he was teasing her. She felt herself blushing.

Skye's eyes were warm and soft as they held hers. After a long moment, he said tenderly, "Thank God for that little parting sermon of yours. It brought me to God the other night while I was looking for Terry."

Joy was speechless. But the joy that leaped into her eyes caused Skye to continue. "And just yesterday Terry told me that our little blonde preacher had also introduced him to Jesus."

"You aren't angry?"

"Angry? No. I'm delighted! Of course, I wouldn't have said that a few days ago," he said wryly. "Now, I need to know something."

"Yes?" Joy asked, mystified.

"How are things between you and Pitman?"

"Between Jeffrey and me?" Joy repeated slowly. "What do you mean?"

Skye looked extremely uncomfortable. He cleared his throat. "I mean — do you care for him?"

"As a dear friend — yes; as a prospective husband — no." Joy answered calmly, but she hoped Skye could not hear her heart pounding.

Skye stood up abruptly. A smile lit his thin face. "That's all I wanted to know. I'll be back tomorrow." He lifted her hand, placed a kiss on the palm and left quickly.

"My-my-my!" Nurse Kelly said from the doorway. "With all this male attention, I believe I'd be slow to get well."

Joy smiled at her dreamily, but she scarcely heard. Bells were ringing somewhere, the most beautiful she had ever heard! And this time she didn't try to silence them. Skye was a Christian.

34

The next morning Joy was both delighted and surprised when Terry came swinging into her room on crutches. Skye, right behind him, grinned and said, "This young man has been giving the doctor such a bad time that he gave him permission to come see you."

Terry's eyes glowed when they saw Joy, but he was suddenly very shy. "Hi," was all he said. Joy noticed that his thin frame was carefully groomed today in dark blue cords and a blue checkered flannel shirt. His fair hair had been cut recently and had a glossy sheen to it.

"Sit down, both of you. Do I get to write my name on your cast?" Joy asked Terry.

"Sure! That cast has to be on there for a bunch of weeks," he said importantly. Skye helped Terry hold his cast up for Joy to sign.

Nurse Kelly pushed chairs up for them

to sit in and then discreetly withdrew with the words, "Dr. Hestley is allowing fifteen minute visits today."

Terry smiled shyly, and then, as if he couldn't keep it in any longer, announced, "We found Mamma's note. It was in a rip in Sparky's side. Mamma said I was Daddy's very own son."

Joy's eyes quickly went to Skye.

But before she or Skye could say anything, Terry added very solemnly, "But Daddy had already told me that I was his son, even if he wasn't my real father. But I'm glad he is, anyway."

Joy felt a mist rise to her eyes.

Suddenly Terry spoke again in a low, tremulous voice, "But he may not want me for a son when he finds out what I did."

Joy protested quickly, "Of course he will!" Hesitating, she asked, "You haven't talked to him about your secret yet then?" Terry looked at her quickly, then darted a glance at his father. Looking back down at his cast, he shook his head slowly.

Skye's dark eyes were intent on his son as he asked quietly, "What did you do, Terry?"

Terry gulped and a fat tear ran down his face as he raised his eyes to meet his father's. He brushed the tear away quickly, and made two starts before he got the first word out. "I-I killed Mamma and Bob!"

Joy drew in her breath sharply. "Why, that's impossible, Terry. They were killed in the plane crash."

Terry glanced quickly at his father's watchful face and then away. "But I made the plane crash," he said miserably.

"How?" Skye's pale face betrayed his emotion.

Terry choked on a sob, then blurted, "Mamma was running away and leaving me so I ran out in front of the plane. I thought they would stop and take me, but t-the plane just ran on around me. T-then it ran off the runway into t-the ditch and crashed into a-a pole." His face had gone ashen. "I k-killed my m-mother." He burst into a torrent of tears.

For a long moment, Skye seemed too stunned to move. Joy opened her mouth to speak, then closed it without a word as she saw Skye move quickly to Terry's chair, kneel and wrap his arms about the desolate child.

For a long poignant moment Skye held Terry close to him; then he held him just far enough away to look into his eyes. Giving him a slight shake, he said clearly, "Terry, listen to me!"

Terry looked at Skye, tears still streaming down his cheeks.

"Terry, you did not cause that plane to crash! A guest told me after the accident that when Bob left the house, he was almost too drunk to walk. Someone would have stopped him but no one dreamed he would try to fly that plane. Two other people said the plane was wobbling all over the runway and almost crashed when it made the sweep to come back for takeoff. You may have run out in its path, but if Bob had not been drunk, he could have kept the accident from happening.

"Do you understand, Terry? You did not wreck that plane! Bob did! Even if he had succeeded in getting the plane in the air, he could never have kept it there. Do you understand, Terry?"

Tears were no longer running from Terry's eyes as he stared unbelievingly at Skye. "Y-you mean I didn't kill Mamma?" He turned incredulous eyes upon Joy and said slowly, "And all this time I thought everyone would hate me and the police would put me in j-jail if I t-told."

"Nothing doing, kid." The tautness had disappeared from Skye's face and he spoke jauntily, "You don't get to be a jailbird after all." He punched Terry lightly on the arm.

Terry's face lit up like the rainbow after a storm.

"Good morning, everyone," a voice said from the doorway. Joy and Skye, totally absorbed in Terry's confession, were both startled as they turned from Terry to see the doctor standing in the doorway. "I'm pleased to see both of my patients doing so well." He moved into the room. "Skye, why don't I examine Terry while you have him here?"

At Skye's nod, Dr. Hestley spoke to Terry, "Come along, young man and I'll show you my examination room. We won't be gone long."

Terry, looking almost like a completely new child, went willingly enough. He liked the doctor.

"I'm so thrilled that things are going well with you and Terry now," Joy said, smiling up at Skye.

"Yes," Skye said gravely. "I'm realizing now that I have never been a real father to Terry. Providing food, clothes and shelter is not all there is to it. You can't imagine the joy I felt when I held my son in my arms — and he was willing to be there. What I have missed all these years! No doubt I'll still make mistakes, but Terry and I will have God to help us now. And

345

we owe it all to you!"

Joy shook her head. "No, you owe it all to the Lord. But I am glad I had a part in it."

For a long moment Skye gazed at her, until she felt the color surging into her face and she looked away in sudden embarrassment and confusion.

"You're the most fantastic woman," he finally said. "You know, I suppose, that I'm in love with you!"

"Y-you are?" His improbable words set her heart to racing.

"I know this is sudden, but I was never more serious in my life."

"S-Skye, you j-just think you love me. I remind you of your dead wife, just as I do Terry."

Skye's dark eyes were warm upon her as he shook his head. "No, it's not that. You are blonde and blue-eyed and so was Lillian. But there the resemblance ends. You are the warm, generous, caring person that she never was. I loved her once but I knew her well. She was much like I was until a few days ago — primarily concerned with gratifying her own desires.

"I know that I am, to a large degree, responsible for the break-up of our marriage. I'm deeply sorry for my part in it, and have told God so. But that is over and past. I

346

can't go back and change anything." His voice was husky with emotion. "But I can go forward — with God. With Him as my helper, I plan to be a real father to Terry."

Skye's voice was warm and vibrant. "And we both need you and want you. Will you marry me?"

When she didn't speak, Skye leaned over and gently laid his lips against hers. "I think I've wanted to do that ever since I first saw you," Skye said softly, "even when I was growling at you."

At Skye's first astonishing words, Joy had felt a bubble of excitement begin to expand in the vicinity of her heart. Now, the bubble seemed to burst, spreading its tingly, deliciously warm, living rays throughout her body.

At last she spoke. "I have to be honest with you, Skye. I don't want to rush into anything. My first marriage was a disaster. I do care about you — and Terry — but we must both be sure."

"I can wait," Skye said. "What I see in your eyes is all I need right now. But I hope I don't have to wait too long."

"Wait for what?" Carole asked innocently, strolling into the room.

Skye stood up and said promptly, "For this good-looking woman to marry me."

Carole's eyes widened as she looked from Skye's warm grey eyes to Joy's shining blue eyes and blushing face. "I'm sorry," she said, backing toward the door. For once the self-assured Carole was embarrassed. "I think I blundered in at the wrong time."

"It's perfectly all right," Skye said. "I had planned to try to properly thank you and David today for all your help in Terry's rescue. Perhaps you would be my guests here tonight for dinner if you don't have other plans. I'd like Jeffrey to come, too."

"We'd love to," Carole said enthusiastically.

"I don't deserve such good friends as you all have been to me," Skye said humbly. "I've been such a fool about so many things, but with God's help, I plan to be a different man."

He turned toward Joy and his voice was husky, "Without even knowing she was doing so, Joy's words helped me find the Lord."

"How marvelous!" Carole said, wonder shining in her soft dark blue eyes.

"Come and sit down, Carole," Joy urged. "You, too, Skye. I'm dying to hear all about Terry's rescue. If Nurse Kelly tries to shoo you out, I'll tell her I *am* resting."

Carole shook her head. "I'll come back a little later. And Skye, if you and Jeffrey will decide on a time for dinner, he can let us know. We'll look forward to seeing you then."

When Carole entered her room in the main part of the lodge a few minutes later, she was still smiling.

"Well," David said, "what are you so pleased about?"

"You'll never guess who I just left holding hands and looking at each other with stars in their eyes," Carole said dreamily. "You know, they do make a striking pair! Skye is so lean and brown, with those piercing grey eyes and dark hair; Joy is blonde, blue-eyed and delicately lovely. I hope she asks me to be her matron of honor!"